Into Thin Air

An Alexander Ranch Matter #2

I0521228

By Marla Josephs

Cover photo by Beverly Fields and Amado Temporal

© Tempfield Press and Beverly Fields 2014

Check out more titles by Marla Josephs at:

www.marlajosephs.com

Chapter 1

I was probably going to get the shit kicked out of me...again, but I wasn't going down without a fight. So far I was holding my own. He sent a combination of strikes my way followed by a spinning kick, but I parried them all adding a strike of my own. I was working up a good sweat. Apparently, he was too because he pulled his shirt off. Distracted by all those toned muscles and that sexy six pack, I caught the next kick directly in the gut. This, not only knocked the wind out of me but, sent me flying into the hard wall. I slumped to the floor, gaping like a fish trying to catch my breath.

"Lela!" yelled Shane, my sparring partner, flying across the room and landing on his knees at my side. "Lela, are you ok?"

I couldn't speak. I could feel my eyes bulging and my head reeling as my inability to obtain oxygen made me light headed. Then, as though my muscles had unclenched, I took in a deep, gasping breath and then another.

"That's it. Deep breaths," Shane encouraged, running his hands along my ribcage checking for damage. I winced and he pulled his hand back sharply. "I am so sorry, sweetheart. I thought you were going to block. Why did you just stand there?"

"I was distracted," I wheezed out, breathing a little better now.

"Distracted?" he looked perplexed. "Distracted by what? There's no one in here but you and I, and nothing in here is distracting."

"You took off your damn shirt," I grumbled.

His gaze lifted from where he was lightly probing my stomach to my face, and a hint of amusement lit under the concern in his eyes.

"So, you got distracted by me taking off my shirt?"

1

"Have you seen your chest? It's darn distracting," I said truthfully. I thought he'd probably done it on purpose. However, his perplexed expression had me rethinking this assumption. He sat back on his heels and looked at me speculatively, a slight grin on his face.

"What?"

"So, is that what I have to do to get your attention? Take off my shirt?" he asked, his face taking on a heated and flirty expression as he ran a finger along my cheek. "If I'd known that, I'd have done it a long time ago."

I struggled up to a full seated position. He wrapped his arm around my back to support me.

"Are you sure you aren't hurt? Can you stand?" he asked, the slight amusement fading. Concern reclaimed control of his features as he watched me struggle up on one knee trying to stand.

"I'm fine," I said, patting him on the check and then pushed myself wobbly to a standing position. He kept his arm around my waist and helped me stand.

"See, I'm fine," I said, looking into his face now with what I hoped was a reassuring smile. The concern was still there, but there was something else too. He still had an arm around me and I was practically flush against his beautifully sculpted, rock hard, bare chest. He was looking at me now with deep speculation. My voice sounded a little breathless when I next spoke and it had nothing to do with the kick to the gut I'd received. "What?"

"So, you were saying something about my bared chest distracting you?" His voice had taken on a husky, teasing tone. I flushed but said nothing. He brushed my hair out of my face with the other hand that wasn't still wrapped around my waist. "I've been wanting to get your attention for a while."

Caught off guard and rendered speechless by mixed emotions, I could do nothing but stare back into his dark, heated eyes. I couldn't deny I was attracted to him. Heck, I'd wanted to get his attention too, but flashes of Jordan always stopped me from acting on it. Wasn't this what I wanted though? A regular relationship with a regular guy? Hadn't I held my attraction and feelings for Jordan in check and distanced myself to give myself a chance at a normal relationship? I did not belong in Jordan's world. I wasn't a member of his superhuman squad. I was just a regular, plain old, human. And, this was a regular, plain old, gorgeous, sweet, charming, human guy. He was stroking my hair now and looking at me with a knowing look.

"The way you're looking at me, I'm getting the impression that I've had your attention and didn't know it. I've wanted to do this for a while," he said closing his hand around my disheveled ponytail and tugging. My head came up as his mouth came down gently and sweetly on mine, and I melted involuntarily into him.

His lips were feather soft at first causing my muscles to relax and little flutters in my tummy. Well, one thing was certain, Shane was no slouch in the kissing department. It was a light, playful kiss. One meant to test my response. He nipped my bottom lip playfully. When I nipped back he pulled me harder against him and deepened the kiss. He teased the corners of my mouth until I sighed with pleasure. He took advantage of my parted lips by slipping his tongue inside and stroking my tongue with his. This kiss was slow, hot and wet and I could do nothing but hold on and enjoy the ride.

"Am I interrupting," came a very deceptively calm voice from the doorway. I jerked in Shane's arms as my body seemed to recognize the voice even before my mind did. The voice was so deceivingly calm and genial that the hint of a threat was all the louder. Shane and I both turned towards the door to see Jordan standing there with an unreadable expression on his face. His face might be unreadable but his eyes were glittering.

Chapter 2

"What are you doing here?" I asked, trying not to flinch from the anger I could feel boring a hole in me. His steely eyes held mine with such intenseness, it was hard not to cower.

"Logan sent me," he said taking a step forward. Shane must have also felt the undercurrent of wrath Jordan brought to the room. He released his hold on my hair and waist and subtly moved protectively in front of me.

Poor Shane. He had no idea that even with his several black belts, he was no match for Jordan. Jordan saw Shane's protective stance. I could tell he was thinking the same thing I was, as an unamused smirk threatened to curl his lip. Jordan was itching for a fight. I touched Shane's arm as I stepped slightly in front of him to face Jordan. I was almost certain Jordan wouldn't hurt me.

"Why didn't he call? And, why didn't you knock?" I asked lifting my chin and forcing a note of challenge in my voice. He had no right to be angry or whatever he was. It wasn't like we were together and I'd been caught cheating on him, even if it did sort of feel that way. I refused to allow him to make me feel as if I were doing something wrong. Besides, he had no right to just walk in my house.

4

"He tried, several times. I guess you were too *busy* to hear your phone," he said, emphasizing the word busy and flicking a glance over Shane.

"Hello," came a feminine voice from beyond the doorway and behind Jordan. Daisy came into view. "Sorry to barge in on you, but no one answered the door and it was unlocked."

My door had not been unlocked. I knew Daisy was trying to calm down what she perceived to be a potentially explosive situation, so I took a deep, calming breath and exhaled. I would not react to Jordan's high handed actions and his attitude that he had the right to enter my house whenever he wanted. Who did he think he was?

Another glance at Daisy's uneasy face had me rechecking my own temper. I'd deal with Jordan later. I'd made it quite clear the day I was almost killed the second time by Kevin, a drainer Jordan had been protecting me from, there would be no more kisses or anything else between us. The only thing I could offer was friendship. He was the one who'd apparently made the decision that friendship wasn't enough and had stayed away from me these last six weeks. I had respected that decision.

My world had been turned upside down and inside out the day I'd stumbled across Ethan in the woods being shot by two goons. Then, I'd basically been taken into protective custody by the Alexanders, only to learn that they were some kind of super human family made up of drainers and healers.

Drainers survived by draining the life force from living things. Bad drainers killed by draining the life force of people and animals completely. Healers were just that, healers. Jordan and his brother Logan were drainers while, Daisy, her sister Grace, and their cousin Ethan, were all healers.

5

Although Jordan and Logan were drainers, they were some of the good guys and actually protected people from their own kind. Through my ordeal with the Alexanders, Jordan and I had found ourselves struggling over a mutual attraction that had involved some very hot and lustful kisses. Though I freely admit I couldn't seem to shake this strong attraction I had for him, I'd decided that getting involved with anyone that wasn't a plain old, normal, human was not in my best interest. And, I'd made that quite clear to him. In response, he had disappeared. I hadn't even seen him in six weeks! Now he wanted to act the part of the injured party? The jerk. It was his fault I was in this situation in the first place.

I'd been doing just fine solo until Jordan had come along with his damn kisses. He'd awaken dormant urges that were plaguing me constantly. Sure, I went on the occasional date here and there. And, I certainly didn't turn down the potentially mind blowing kisses that came with those occasional dates. Still, I hadn't had any desire to do the relationship thing. I definitely had never found myself so instantly and strongly attracted to anyone before.

Relationships were just too much work and too complicated for me right now. And since I just couldn't bring myself to do the casual thing, or friends with benefits thing, I tended to keep to myself. Not being overly social and having a job that kept me extremely busy also helped. Everything was flowing just fine…before Jordan. Post Jordan had me feeling like a ball of lustful hormones more often than not. Something had to be done, and I was just beginning to think Shane might be able to be that easy something.

"Shane, it's so nice to see you again," Daisy was saying, as she breezed into the room and stopped in front of Shane, extending a hand to him. Unlike Jordan, Daisy had been around during the last six weeks, as had Ethan. She'd even participated in some of my sparring sessions with Shane.

"Good to see you too, Daisy," he said, returning her greeting warmly if not a bit stiffly. He grasped her hand gently but never quite took his attention from Jordan's stony countenance.

"What's going on, Daisy?" I asked, ignoring Jordan.

"Something's come up, and Logan would like to talk to you as soon as possible. I don't know all of the details. Logan wanted you in on the meeting."

I could read between the lines. For Logan to actually send for me, it had to be serious. I knew they wouldn't tell me anything in front of Shane though.

"Do I have time to take a shower?" I asked hopefully. Shane and I had been sparring for over an hour and I was pretty sweaty.

"Of course," Daisy assured me as Jordan removed himself from the doorway and turned to face the wall. He stared intently down at some practice weapons by the door.

"I'm sorry," I said turning to Shane.

"No problem. Our session was up anyway," he said easily. Then, his face grew serious as he glanced at Jordan and then back at me and lowered his voice in concern, "Are you going to be ok? Do you want me to stay with you?"

"I'll be fine." I gave him an appreciative smile for his concern. He looked into my eyes for a long moment as if trying to ascertain the truth of my statement in them. Satisfied he nodded. "Ok. Call me tonight, alright?"

"I promise."

He gave me a quick kiss on my forehead and headed for the door.

"I'll walk you out," Daisy said following Shane out the door and past Jordan. The moment they were out the door, Jordan turned to face me.

"What the hell is going on between the two of you?" he demanded in a low steely voice.

"None of your business, Jordan," I shot back evenly as I tried to brush past him. He grabbed my arm. Seriously? Did he really think he had the right to come in here and act all caveman?

"The hell it isn't," he growled, glaring down at me.

"Jordan, I don't have time for this. If Logan sent you guys to get me then it must be urgent, and I need a shower," I replied calmly but sternly. He released me and his hand flew up with a growl of frustration. I flinched back reflexively and my arm went up protectively to block a blow. Jordan froze with his hand halfway through his hair and stared at me in surprise which, quickly turned to outrage.

"Did you think I was going to hit you?" His voice was full of incredulity. I raised my chin defiantly but didn't answer. He shook his head slowly with a look of shocked disbelief on his face that rapidly turned to disgust.

It was a damn reflex, but I wasn't going to sit here and defend myself verbally to him. Jordan irate was enough to make anyone flinch. He turned without another word and walked from the room. Daisy entered and grimaced as she saw me sag against the wall.

"Well, that went well," I breathed sarcastically.

"I am so sorry, Lela," Daisy said, her voice full of apology. "We just heard what sounded like a body hitting a wall and you groan. We thought you were being attacked or something. I had no idea you were sparring with Shane. And I didn't know you two were…well, involved or whatever."

"Why would I be being attacked? And, didn't you see his car?"

"Actually I didn't see his car until I just walked him to it just now. He's parked down the street some," she shrugged. "And, I don't know why you'd be being attacked. I just know what I heard, what we both heard, and we reacted. I'm so sorry. I had no idea you guys were becoming more than sparring partners. I wouldn't have been so alarmed and confused when we realized it was Shane's voice we heard in here with you."

"I didn't know we were becoming more than sparring partners either," I mumbled wryly.

"You'd better get in the shower. You're still coming with us to see Logan, right?"

"Yes, of course."

Chapter 3

I took a quick shower and threw on jeans and a t-shirt. I wanted to wear shorts, but I didn't know what I would have to deal with once the Alexanders got ahold of me. I figured jeans were safer. I threw my wet, unruly curls into a ponytail and headed out the door. I jumped into the back seat since Jordan was at the wheel. There was no way I was going to sit next to Jordan all the way to the ranch. Too awkward.

Though I had made it quite clear I didn't want to pursue anything more than friendship with Jordan, being caught kissing Shane did feel a bit like being caught cheating now with Jordan sitting up front all stiff and stony-faced silence. Jordan had said he'd accepted and respected my decision and would give me space and not pursue it further. I hadn't even seen Jordan since that conversation. Daisy and Ethan were always around.

We hung out together watching television, going to dinner or lunch, and even the gym. Jordan had been utterly and completely absent.

Logan and Grace, Jordan's brother and sister in law, had even called to see how I was doing and had invited me over on numerous occasions, but I'd always found an excuse not to come. Since Jordan made it clear by his absence and silence that if he couldn't have more than friendship he didn't want anything at all, I didn't feel it was right to invade his space and home to visit his brother and sister in law. He was keeping his distance, so I felt it was only right for me to honor his decision and also stay away. I could give him that. Being just friends was either an idea he needed to get used to or wasn't interested in. Either way, it was his choice to make.

I had missed him greatly and often wondered if I was making a mistake by rejecting this attraction we had for each other. But, each time I examined the situation I felt sure I was doing the right thing. People walked around every day not knowing anything about this world of super human drainers and healers. I used to be one of those people before being in the wrong place at the wrong time. My life hadn't been quite the same since. However, just because I knew about it didn't mean I should allow myself to become part of it so intimately. It wasn't my world. I was just a regular person trying to live. Jumping into this other reality would surely be madness. And I liked peacefulness too much to deliberately invite madness and chaos into my cozy, peaceful life.

"You're awfully quiet," Daisy said, pulling me from my thoughts as Jordan parked the car in front of the main house on the ranch.

"I'm fine, Daisy."

She didn't look convinced but didn't say anything more. If she thought I was going to open the door to Jordan's anger by discussing it with her in front of him, she was crazy. She must have thought about this too, because she gave Jordan a quick glance before rolling her eyes and opening her door.

We got out of the car and I followed her up the stairs to the main entrance, leaving Jordan in the car. Hearing Jordan's car door slam behind us, I left the entryway door open for him as Daisy and I entered. Once inside she led me to Logan's study. This was the last room I'd been in when I was here last. Logan was seated behind his big desk and rose with a smile at our entrance.

"Lela," he exclaimed and came around the desk to give me a warm hug. "I was beginning to worry that we wouldn't see you again. Thanks so much for coming."

"No problem. It's good to see you too, Logan," I smiled, returning his warm embrace. He really was like a big brother. "So, what's going on that you sent your goons after me?"

"Well," he chuckled at my teasing and his handsome smile reminded me of his recalcitrant brother when he wasn't brooding, "we've got a case I'm hoping you can help us with, but there are some things we need to discuss first."

His face had taken on a more businesslike expression as he turned to Daisy. "Daisy, can you have everyone assemble in the conference room now that Lela is here?"

Daisy nodded and headed out the door.

"Are you ok?" he asked scrutinizing my face. "I'm assuming since you and Daisy arrived without Jordan, he came back in one of those moods you seem to bring out in him. He didn't do anything I'm going to have to pay for did he?"

"No," I smiled sheepishly. "I'm afraid he's a little put out with me though, as usual."

"And let me guess, you don't want to talk about it right?"

"Right."

He gazed up at the ceiling as if seeking patience and sighed, "That's fine. I'm sure I don't want to know anyway. Just answer one question."

"What's that?"

"If you decide to work this case with us, would whatever the problem is between you two now prevent you from being able to work together?"

"I have no problem working with Jordan if he doesn't have a problem working with me," I answered honestly.

"That's basically what he said before he left to go get you. Well, I guess we'll see." He gestured to the door, "Let's head over to the conference room."

So, Logan was aware that Jordan and I were keeping our distance. And, he probably knew why Jordan had decided friendship was not enough. I wanted to ask him what he knew but didn't dare. Not that he'd tell me anyway, even if I asked. But, I wouldn't drag him into this. In the six weeks since I'd last seen and talked to Jordan, no one had mentioned him to me or around me. It was as though everyone carefully avoided the subject of me and Jordan.

Jordan, Grace, Ethan, and Daisy were already in the conference room when Logan and I arrived. Ethan and Grace both jumped up to give me hugs.

"It's so good to see you," Grace beamed giving me a squeeze.

"Hey beautiful," Ethan said, pulling me into his arms after Grace released me and then gave me a loud smacking kiss on the side of my mouth. He glanced at Jordan grinning mischievously, but Jordan sat impassively appearing outwardly calm and not even looking in my direction. He was staring intently down at a blank notebook.

"Let's get started," Logan ordered heading for the front of the room. Everyone returned to their chairs and I took one as far away from Jordan as possible. "Lela, I'll fill you in on what everyone else already knows. We're here to discuss how to proceed on this new case. Our plan of action, however, will be partly determined by whether or not you decide to take this case or not. Of course we hope that you will want to help, but don't feel obligated. Whatever you decide is perfectly fine, as usual. We respect your decision, ok?"

I couldn't help thinking that Jordan rarely respected my decisions. "Sure, ok."

"We've just caught a case regarding the kidnapping of an investment banker. There was no sign of forced entry, or entry period. The man just seems to have vanished in the night. Our preliminary investigation of the property showed the sophisticated alarm system had been expertly bypassed and somehow the man was taken from his bed without his wife's knowledge. She woke up to find him gone with no trace of where or how. So now it's up to us to find him.

"Ok," I interrupted slowly trying to understand. "I don't understand how I can help."

"Well, while we don't know exactly where he is, we strongly suspect there are drainers involved. We have a few people in custody that we have to interview, and we'd like you to be there when we do. We're hoping you can pick up on their feeling and thoughts to give us more answers than their words will."

He was watching me closely as he spoke, as was everyone else in the room. I was starting to get the feeling that there was more to this and I wasn't necessarily going to like it.

"If you don't know how someone got in or out, and there's no sign of forced entry, why do you think he was kidnapped? Maybe he just left."

"When the wife woke up and found her husband missing, she also found a ransom note on the pillow next to her," Grace explained.

"I take it that since you suspect drainers are involved, these people you want to interview are drainers?" I asked still waiting for the other shoe to drop. Something was up.

"Yes," Logan said gravely.

I couldn't help the shutter that ran through me at the very thought. "So, you want me to sit in a room with a drainer while you interrogate him or her?"

"No," Logan answered quickly. "We think that you can listen and watch from the observation room." A pained look came over Logan's face but he continued, "When you were kidnapped, you were able to send clear messages to us all from quite a distance. We're hoping that listening and observing from another room will be just as easy for you and will offer added protection for you as well."

"Why aren't the police handling this, because of the drainers?" I asked.

"Partly," Daisy answered. "The ransom note did more than just demand 20 million dollars be delivered in seven days. It also said that if the wife got the authorities involved, they would kill her husband and then come and take her daughters next. Her daughters are five and seven."

14

Good lord, this poor woman must be going crazy. I could only imagine her terror. As much as I wanted no part of being anywhere near a crazed drainer, I couldn't in good conscience say no if I could help bring this man back to his family. I took a deep breath and tried not to think too hard about what I was about to commit myself to doing.

"I'll do it. But, how do you already have someone to interview if you don't know who's behind all of this?"

"Take some time to think about it before you agree," Logan cautioned. "We still have more to tell you and details to discuss, such as, we're offering a minimum of seven thousand dollars for your services should you decide to help us with this case."

I blinked. "Seven thousand dollars just to listen in and observe your interrogation of a drainer?"

"Well, actually for a week of your services. We will likely have other people to interview and will be working around the clock. We only have less than seven days now. The clock is ticking," Logan clarified.

"Still, seven thousand is a lot of money for a week's worth of work," I responded with disbelief.

Logan's mouth twitched as if he wanted to smile, but he didn't, "Are you really arguing about how much we've decided to pay you?"

"No. I guess not," I chuckled uneasily and shook my head. "I've learned arguing with you people is futile."

"There's more that you need to consider before you agree to this, Lela," Grace said seriously. Now, she was giving me the same worried look that everyone else was. Everyone was now looking at me with varying degrees of concern. Everyone except Jordan. Jordan had been staring intently at the wall in front of him, his notepad, or anything but me. Now he sat looking down at the table with his hands steepled in front

15

of him. I swallowed and nodded, knowing whatever they were going to tell me next was what was causing all the worried and grave looks directed at me. I returned my gaze to Grace. "The person we have to interrogate is Kevin White. We have reason to believe his organization is behind this."

I went stiff as stone and could do nothing but stare at her as ice shards seemed to prick all over my skin. Kevin was dead, wasn't he? My blood froze and felt like ice in my veins. I began to feel slightly dizzy. No one spoke. They all watched my involuntary responses as I stared back at them in horror.

"Lela, you are under no obligation. You can say no," Logan finally broke the silence in a soft, comforting tone.

"But...but, Kevin is dead, right?" I heard myself saying.

"Well, if Jordan had been allowed to keep pummeling the guy he would be, but no. He's not dead," Ethan said gently.

"But, how? Why?" I was sputtered in shock and disbelief. They had told me I was safe. How could I be safe if Kevin was still alive and free to kill me?

"Well, we generally don't kill suspects unless we have to. We capture them," Logan said cautiously. "This is what we do. This is our job."

I just stared at him. I seemed to be being struck dumb frequently today. My mind was whirling trying to make sense of this latest news. This was actually a common occurrence whenever I was around the Alexanders. There was always something unreal going on around them.

Kevin was alive. Why had I assumed Kevin was dead? No one had ever told me that he was dead. They'd just said I was safe. Now I was learning that Kevin, the drainer that had tried to kill me twice, was alive

16

and they wanted me to get close enough to him to hear and observe him and try to read his thoughts and feelings? Seriously?

I looked over at Jordan and noticed his mouth was pinched tightly as if he were determined to keep it shut. Jordan, who had definitely been out for Kevin's blood to protect me, was determined to stay mute now. Maybe he was mad enough at me now to wish he'd let Kevin kill me. Me, who repaid him by fighting my attraction to him and rejecting his feelings for me. Gosh, what could he possibly be thinking right now? By how tightly he was pursing his lips together, it didn't appear that I would be finding out his thoughts on the current topic any time soon.

"Think about it for a while and let us know," Grace instructed. "We know this is a lot for you to consider."

I closed my eyes and dropped my head back, knowing I couldn't say no. A man was out there being held hostage. A wife was worried sick about her husband and her kids were missing their father. I fought through the shivers and the waves of fear that urged me to run. The Alexanders would keep me safe. I had to believe that. They would all keep me safe. Well, everyone except Jordan. At the moment, I got the feeling he hated me and felt a sharp pain in my chest. I wanted, no needed, to know what he was thinking now. But, he hadn't spoken a word to me since he'd walked away from me in disgust from my workout room. No, I wouldn't be getting comfort or advice from that quarter. I refocused on the problem at hand. A man's life, and possibly that of his children, were on the line here. If I could help, how could I say no? How could I not at least try?

"I'll do it," I sighed.

"Are you sure, Lela?" Logan asked frowning with concern. "Time is of the essence, but you should think this over for at least a little while longer."

"I'm sure, Logan," I responded, looking directly into his eyes and locking down any remaining fear. "I'm in."

"Ok," Logan softly agreed after a long assessment. "We need to interrogate Kevin as soon as possible. First, however, there are some things we need to do to mask your scent. And while you are in the observation room, we want you to remain quiet. Remember people like us have better than exceptional hearing. We would prefer he not know you are there. Your little gift is something we want to keep a secret, as I'm sure you do too. We want your gift to be our secret weapon. And, I think it's safer for you all the way around that no one know about it that doesn't need to know. Daisy and Grace will help you with masking your scent. When you are ready, we'll head out."

My scent? I hadn't even thought of that. Yep, I was certifiably crazy. I was going to put myself in reach of someone with super human hearing, smelling, and strength, and who'd tried to kill me...twice.

Chapter 4

Daisy and Grace masked my scent by making me wear their jeans and shirts they'd worn all day. They even made me wear Daisy's riding hat that she used when riding at the ranch. I looked like a fashion misfit by the time they were done with me and we were on our way. I tried not to think too much about wearing someone else's dirty clothes. Granted, they weren't covered in filth or anything. In truth, they weren't dirty at all. They were just previously worn...without being washed. No matter how I tried to spin it, the idea still sort of grossed me out. So I settled on, if it kept me safe from Kevin detecting me, then it was worth it. Besides, Grace had assured me that they'd only worn them for a while around the house to ensure their own scent was infused in the clothing just in case I agreed to work the case with them. I wasn't sure I believed her, but I chose to not question it.

Kevin was being held in a facility for extremely dangerous criminals. At least, that was the official story. In fact, this was a facility for holding the likes of criminal drainers along with extremely dangerous criminals just to make it legit. Few government officials knew of the drainers and healers, and the majority that did were healers and drainers themselves posing as regular humans. Most others only knew that they were basically a deep cover, black ops unit that hid in plain sight. They had their own unit within the facility and even the people who worked in other departments weren't aware that they were more than regular old humans in the wing with the highest clearance. Everyone who worked there was hand-picked. There were other drainers and healers working all over the facility, but only drainers and healers worked in the area where Kevin and other criminals of the super human variety were being held.

When I entered the observation room, the interrogation room on the other side of the glass was still empty. I glanced around the observation room I was currently in to find it was filled with what looked like blankets and clothes that were obviously from the dirty laundry. Great. Another reminder that I was wearing other people's unwashed clothes. Again, nothing was covered with filth, but I could smell ranch smells mixed with the varying colognes, perfumes and body washes of the Alexander clan. It wasn't an unpleasant smell. In fact, it was oddly familiar. Ok, better to focus on the task at hand.

I was standing a few steps back from the mirror looking into the empty room when Jordan came and stood beside me a few steps away.

"You might want to sit down," he suggested in a murmured voice. These were the first words he'd said to me since storming angrily out of my house. His demeanor was all business and indifference, not a hint of any emotion or familiarity. I wasn't sure how I felt about this although it left an uncomfortable tightness in my stomach. "This may take a while."

"How long do you think it will take?" I asked trying to adopt his low, quiet whisper and indifference.

He shrugged, "Knowing Logan, he'll try to keep it as short as possible for your sake. He knows this tires you out. Still, we need to find Mr. Beck as quickly as possible. You might as well be comfortable regardless."

"Why are you whispering?" I questioned, whispering back.

"This room is sound proofed from the rest of the building. As long as we keep our voices to a whisper, even other drainers and healers can't hear us in the rest of the building. However, once someone enters the interrogation room, anyone with the hearing sensitivity of a drainer or healer can hear whatever is said in this room, even a whisper. So no speaking once the door opens."

I glanced at one of the stools siting in the room but shook my head. I was too nervous to sit. I could feel Jordan watching me, but I couldn't deal with him right now. I needed to concentrate on the job I was asked to do and focus on not freezing in terror, or running from the room screaming like a loon once Kevin entered the room.

"Lela?" Jordan's voice was barely a whisper. I turned to look at him, ready to shut him down if he wanted to resume the Shane issue, but his face was not angry. Well, not entirely angry. His face was still tight but his eyes seemed to hold some anguish and frustration that kept me from speaking.

"I want to apologize for barging in on you and the way I behaved," he continued. "I heard the sound of a struggle when we arrived.

I heard a hard thump against a wall and your gasp. And, well, I sort of panicked. Then, when I came in and saw…, I'm just sorry. I shouldn't have reacted that way."

His words were sincere, even if a little brittle around the edges. I knew it took a lot for him to say them and I felt myself softening towards him. I gave him a nod but my face was too stiff to smile. I'm sure I looked rigid because I sure felt rigid. I took a deep breath to try and relax.

"Are you really up for this?" he asked, apprehension radiating from him and breaking through his indifferent manner.

"As ready as I'll ever be," I uttered back.

We both turned towards the glass as the doors of the interrogation room opened and Logan entered with Ethan and Kevin. Kevin's hands were chained in front of him. I shuttered at the sight and felt Jordan move closer to my side. He looked so normal and harmless yet, I knew just how vicious he really was. The memories of what I had gone through at the hands of that monster threatened to flood into my mind and take it hostage. I held them back. I could not go there. I could not think of all the terror and fear he had caused me.

Kevin took a seat facing the glass and looked directly at it. I stiffened. A slow, arrogantly challenging grin appeared on his face as he seemed to look directly at me. I was instantly immobilized and rigid with fear. He could see me! I was sure of it. A slow, cold smile spread across his face chilling me to the bone and causing my skin to prickle. The next thing I knew Jordan grabbed me and had me pinned against the wall next to the glass, out of Kevin's view. He had my face firmly cradled in his big hands forcing my gaze to his and staring intently into my eyes.

"*Breath before you pass out,*" his voice sounded in my head. Then he picked me up and carried me out and down a long hallway to another room. Daisy had met us in the hall and followed behind us. I belatedly realized that there were other people milling around in other offices along the hall who glanced up and watched as Jordan whisked me down the hallway.

"What happened?" Daisy asked, following us into an empty room and closing the door behind her. I focused on her now and the sound of her agitated voice.

"She just froze up and started holding her breath when Kevin entered. I think she was getting ready to pass out," Jordan responded to Daisy in hushed tones before turning back to me. "Breath, Lela. Take deep breaths. That's it."

"I was not going to pass out," I said a little drunkenly. "I've never passed out in my life until I met you Alexanders."

Daisy and Jordan just exchanged worried looks. The light-headed feeling was receding and I was beginning to feel more normal, well except for the gripping fear.

"Two-way glass," Jordan said with a frown, as if just coming to some conclusion. "He looked directly at us and smiled."

"He couldn't really see her though, surely," Daisy said in disbelief. "And the lights weren't on in the observation room."

"I don't think he could make her out clearly but we were rather close to the glass. Even though regular people can't see, one of us would be able to see more."

Daisy frowned in thought for a moment and then turned to me. "He could likely make out some shadows. I think he was just trying to intimidate whomever was behind the glass. He knows he's being observed. Are you ok, Hun?"

"He looked right at me, Daisy," I wheezed.

22

"I know," she said placing an arm around my shoulders. "But, I'm certain he doesn't know who you are. Try to take deep breaths and relax."

I closed my eyes and breathed deeply. After a few moments my breathing calmed and I regained control of myself. I opened my eyes to see Jordan's tight jaw, his indifference gone. Though, his current expression was not so easy to read.

"Better?" Daisy asked.

I nodded.

"Do you actually need to see Kevin to read him? That is, if you are still willing to do this," Daisy queried thoughtfully.

"I don't know," I answered, sounding a bit breathy but calmer than I felt. "I don't think so."

They both looked at me a little confused.

"If I can read him, I mean," I clarified. "I don't see why I would need to see him. I'd rather not."

"I'm thinking that if you sit or stand along the wall of the observation room next to the glass, you will be out of Kevin's view and he out of yours. Jordan and I both will stay in the room with you."

"I can try," I reassured her. I could do this. I could at least see if I could read him.

"Let me tell Logan and Ethan that we can start again in a moment," Daisy said stepping out of the room. She came right back after a minute or two. Moments later I was being led back out into the hall by Jordan where Grace was giving directions to what looked like a few guards.

"*Are you ok?*" her voice sounded in my head. I gave her a steady nod and headed back down the hall to the observation room. I walked in and sat on a stool that had been placed by the wall. I leaned my back against the wall next to the glass and turned to watch Daisy. She was standing in front of the window. Jordan placed his hands gently on my shoulders and began to massage.

"Just keep breathing. When you're ready, see what you can sense from the other room," came Jordan's voice in my head again. I closed my eyes and opened my senses. I could feel curiosity, derision, and boredom coming from the other room.

"I'm ready," I thought to Jordan. He nodded to Daisy and she stepped to the door, opened it and gave a thumbs up to someone then closed the door and returned to the window. A moment later Ethan and Logan entered the room. I was surprised that I could identify beyond a doubt each of their minds as they entered the room and whose feelings and thoughts I was reading. I couldn't see them, but I'd felt them enter the room and could identify them as if I had seen them.

Ethan was feeling concern and confusion, and animosity towards Kevin. Belatedly I realized his concern and confusion were for me. He didn't know what had happened. There were very few actual words in his mind, but his emotions or feelings, along with the few words that entered his mind, had me reading him rather well.

"I'm fine, Ethan. Everything is fine," I thought to him and felt him relax with relief. *"Now focus."*

At my reassurance and gentle command, his mind began to refocus on the task at hand.

"Yes ma'am," came his mental response and I could almost see him smile.

Next, I turned my attention to Logan. He too was concerned but better at compartmentalizing his thoughts and emotions. His feelings of concern were completely separated and in the background, while his concentration and attention on the coming interrogation were front and center. Their minds were so fascinatingly different and individual, just like looking at a face. Only there was so much more detail available from reading a mind.

Now that I'd gotten my bearings, I turned my attention to Kevin. The first thing I noticed with relief was, I wasn't sensing any evidence that Kevin knew who was behind the glass. He was wondering what the holdup was and why the interrogation seemed to be delayed. It made him nervous. That went a long way in relieving my mind. Focusing my attention on Ethan and Logan had awakened my curiosity and fascination. And, while I still felt fear, I didn't feel panic over feeling Kevin's mind. I was actually surprised that Kevin's mind seemed so normal.

I guess I had been expecting to see a twisted, evil, and demented mind. However, at first glance, his mind seemed to be quite normal and even sane. I made a writing gesture and Jordan stepped away for a moment. He stepped back to me and put pen and paper in my hand. I began writing what I felt emanating from the monster in the next room. His mind may not appear to be that of a deranged lunatic, but he was still a monster to me.

I was only writing words that described the exact feeling or emotion I was able to pick up. The words were in no order or sentence structure that would have made any sense. I figured I could explain everything later. For now, it was more important to capture what I could.

I wrote the words *confused, apprehension,* and *curious,* because that's what Kevin was feeling. Logan had begun asking questions, but Kevin was ignoring him. He'd asked seemingly unnecessary questions, about who was working for him and what his full name was. I was confused at first and my mind went to Logan's. Immediately I sensed that Logan was

25

asking preliminary test questions for me to have a baseline, just as one would do with a lie detector test. I smiled. I was a human lie detector. I allowed myself a few seconds to muse over this and then refocused on the task at hand. My mind immediately swung back to Kevin's and I felt a little light headed, as if I had stood up too fast. I'd have to keep my focus on Kevin. Jumping around would take too much energy. It didn't take long before the questions began to change.

"What do you know about the kidnapping of an investment banker last night?" Logan asked in the same boring tone he'd been using. Suddenly Kevin was alert. He was still confused but alert.

"How could I know anything? I'm locked up in here?" Kevin's voice held a bored and slightly irritated tone, but he was definitely alert now.

"So, you're telling me you don't know anything about the disappearance of an investment banker named Wallace Beck?" Ethan took up the questioning.

This time Kevin mentally started. I continued scribbling the words of the feelings and thoughts that came to me. Logan and Ethan continued asking basic questions regarding the kidnapping. I could feel Kevin's confusion deepen and him trying to figure out what Logan and Ethan were talking about from their questions. He didn't know anything about the kidnapping. That was clear. But, he did know who the victim was. Hopefully that was something. I wasn't feeling like I had helped much, when all I could tell them was Kevin didn't know much. I was relieved when Logan brought the interview to a close. I was getting just as frustrated as Kevin felt.

All in all, the interview was thankfully very short. Once Kevin was removed from the room, I sagged with relief.

"Are you ok?" Jordan asked coming around to face me.

"I'm fine. I'm just tired." I was feeling better than I thought I would though. Opening my senses like that was exhausting but also exhilarating. Not having a purpose to use my gift, I'd always tried to keep my senses closed so I didn't have to hear anyone's thoughts. I had no idea how fascinating it would feel to be able to use it in such a way.

Moments later the whole Alexander clan was crowding into the little observation room. I had to reassure them over and over again that I was fine. They were a fussy bunch. I'd have to talk to them about toning that down a bit. They were all a bit overprotective. I really was fine, a little frazzled after the fact, but fine. I was enthralled at how much and what I was able to do. That fascination helped to curb the fear and other feelings, allowing me to focus.

"Were you able to get anything?" Daisy asked, refocusing everyone after they were satisfied I wasn't damaged for life in some way.

"Actually, I was." I smiled, feeling a bit smug at how I'd been able to really get into Kevin's mind. Then I frowned. "I'm just not sure how much help it will be."

"Can it wait until we get back to the ranch?" Jordan interrupted. "I'd prefer to get her as far from here as possible."

"I agree," Logan nodded, his concern coming to the front of his mind now that his task of interrogation was complete. I hadn't realized I was still feeling their moods. I closed down my senses.

Chapter 5

"Kevin was genuinely confused," I was saying after being whisked away and placed front and center in the conference room back at the ranch. All eyes were on me, which normally was something I didn't like.

27

However, having lead many a staff meeting at Hanley's, this oddly felt like just another staff meeting. Though, the subject matter was far more exciting.

"So, he didn't know anything?" Logan asked sounding a little disappointment.

"Not exactly," I answered, trying to tamp down my own disappointment that I wasn't able to help more. "I sensed that he didn't know anything about the kidnapping, but I think he knew the victim. I was sensing boredom, mild curiosity, and amusement before you mentioned Wallace Beck's name. When you said that name he immediately started paying attention. Yet, he became even more confused."

"Hm, I'm not sure what to make of that," Ethan interjected thoughtfully.

"Me neither, except it made me think he must know the victim. And there's more. I could sense him trying to get information from the questions you guys were asking. Even though the confusion never left him, he started getting angry. I got the feeling that he was suspecting something was afoot but didn't know what it was. His mind was moving so fast though, he never really came to any conclusion. It was as though he was trying to figure something out."

"Interesting," Logan added also looking thoughtful. "How tired are you from this ordeal."

"I'm ok."

"Are you up to doing it again? I hate to ask. But, as you know, time is of the essence."

Grace spoke before I could respond, "You want to interview Kevin again?"

"No, I want to ask Mrs. Beck if she knows Kevin," Logan explained. "I don't doubt her innocence and distress over her husband's abduction, but what if she knows Kevin? It could shed more light on what's going on here if she does. And, it doesn't hurt to make sure that she isn't keeping anything from us. After all, Lela wasn't there when we interviewed her before, and none of *us* are mind readers. We need to use all the resources we have if we are going to beat the clock on this one."

Thirty minutes later we were pulling into the Beck's driveway. The house was a two story Spanish style home that sat back from a tree lined street. It had been a quiet ride. I sat in the back seat saying nothing while Logan and Jordan exchanged few words in the front. I'd leaned my head back on the seat and closed my eyes to try and rest a little. Too soon, Jordan was opening my door for me and leading me up the stairs to the front door like the gentleman he was. His countenance, however, had returned to all business mode.

Moments later we were led into a small siting room where a plump, dark haired woman sat with a faraway gaze. She looked up and I could see her pretty features were strained with stress, her eyes red from a night of crying. She stood and gave us a wobbly smile. I wouldn't have considered Mrs. Beck overweight. She just wasn't thin. She had nice round curves, a small waist and an overall attractive figure that would definitely catch a man's attention. I found myself watching Jordan and Logan to see their reactions to her. Despite her obvious distress, Mrs. Beck was a beautiful woman. And, her tear stained face and watery green gold eyes made her even more attractive. But, the only thing that seemed to be awakened in both of the Alexander brothers was their sense of chivalry.

"Thank you so much for seeing us, Mrs. Beck," Logan was saying and clasping her delicate hands comfortingly in his large ones. I don't think he realized the look of sympathy he was giving her was one that would warm up a woman's libido under less dire circumstances. However, I was sensing nothing but sympathetic attentiveness from Logan and Jordan and hopeful relief from Mrs. Beck. Seeing them gave her hope.

"Anything I can do," she smiled back at him with her watery eyes.

"This won't take long. We only have a couple of questions for you," Logan said. "Have you thought of anything new about what happened last night?"

"No. Nothing," she replied sounding more distressed. "I've told you everything I remember."

"That's fine," Logan reassured her patting her hands and then released them. "Just let us know if you think of anything else that you may not have thought of before."

"Why don't we sit," Jordan suggested.

"Yes, of course," Mrs. Beck replied sounding flustered. "I'm so sorry."

Jordan introduced me, and then Mrs. Beck gestured us all to seats.

"We wanted to ask you if you knew someone by the name of Kevin white," Logan asked, once we were all seated.

She frowned in confusion. I could feel her searching her brain for some possible connection. "I don't know that name. Should I?"

"No," Logan assured her. "It's just a name that came up."

"Does this Kevin White have something to do with my husband's abduction?" she asked anxiously, still trying to find some connection or memory.

"We think he may be involved but we aren't sure how. Don't worry yourself. We weren't expecting you to know who he is," Jordan explained. "We are just crossing every T and dotting every I. We have several other leads and teams investigating."

"Oh. Ok," she said quietly. I could sense her feeling of despair. I closed my senses before I was brought to tears by the overwhelming crush of her emotions. Logan clearly could read them on her face. He retook her hands in his and looked into her eyes.

"Mrs. Beck, don't worry. We have several leads. And, we are working around the clock to bring your husband home safely."

She nodded and lifted her chin.

Chapter 6

A total of six and a half hours from the time Jordan and Daisy barged into my house, Jordan was driving me home. This felt like the longest Sunday of my life. They'd come to my house around three in the afternoon and it was now nine-thirty in the evening. Despite the sun just going down on what had been a gorgeous summer day, I was wiped out. After an unfruitful but quick stop at Wallace Beck's house to speak to his wife, I was taken back to the ranch where they fed me while I told them the wife did not know who Kevin was. Kevin White, as the Alexander's knew him from his employment records, probably didn't exist. I found it strange that an investigative firm would have hired such a person. But, I was assured that it was common to have aliases among their kind. It was necessary even. My mind wondered from Kevin and the case to thoughts of Jordan.

I'd worked very hard to keep my mind off of Jordan and the tension between us. Yea, he'd apologized earlier and had been attentive throughout the interviews, but that was all business. Now that there was nothing to do with the case but wait, I most certainly hadn't wanted to find myself alone with Jordan, let alone in such a confined space as a car.

However, I hadn't wanted to bring attention to my discomfort or give the impression I couldn't work with him when he offered to drive me home. He had walked me to the waiting SUV with a gentle hand at my back after the interrogation with Kevin. He'd opened my door and then squeezed in beside me in the back seat. Logan had taken the driver's seat and Grace sat beside him. I'd been shaking a little, probably from the combination of fear and excitement. I'd definitely felt like I was coming down from an adrenaline rush. Jordan had glanced over at me, put his arm around my shoulders and pulled me into his side without a word. And, I willingly buried myself there, feeling guiltier over the incident earlier in the day with Shane that he'd walked in on. I'd begun to doubt my own conviction of denying my feelings for him, and his for me, in my quest for a normal life in the face of his solid support. I was calm by the time I'd arrived at the ranch for the first debriefing.

When I was with Jordan, everything seemed right. Well, everything except being chased, kidnapped, and almost killed by a super human. But, that wasn't all the time. It wasn't even most of the time. Then again, how many times did one have to be almost killed before common sense told them that hanging around dangerous company could have dangerous results? But, now that I was in the car with him…alone, all the tension from earlier seemed to return. He hadn't said anything to me, and I hadn't uttered a word to him. It was not a companionable silence. I let out a sigh and saw Jordan glance at me, but he didn't say anything. My mind was going around in circles, as usual when it came to Jordan. I guess my feelings for him and my need for normalcy would always be at odds. And that was why I'd made the decision to go no further than friendship.

I had a hard enough time having relationships with regular people. They tended to be needy and always taking but never give anything in return. I couldn't count the times my so called "friends" cried on me about their frivolous woes. But, when I needed someone to talk to, they were always too busy or found some way to not be available. Being told what a great listener you were or how great the advice you gave was didn't make for a good friend. My brother, Blake, had been the only one who'd always been there for me. Even if he didn't always know exactly what to do or have all the answers, he was always there. And, I'd always tried to do the same for him.

Of course, our parents had a lot to do with our emotional standoffishness. They were never there for us emotionally. We learned very early that they were not going to be there for us emotionally and the most important duty was holding up the pretty little image and lie that our family, especially my mother, was perfect. It was surprising how many people actually bought the lie.

Our mother always wanted us to listen to her lament about this or that, but couldn't be bothered to hear us, though in her own brain somehow she did. My mother put on a great show though. She could be very sweet and always had an ear to lend to someone else. Everyone thought she was just the kindest, most giving person. And, she was to everyone else. However, she loved talking about how stupid or pitiful they were behind their backs once they told her all of their business. She would talk about it to certain people not all. Wouldn't want to ruin her image and all. But, mostly, she wanted to bombard me with it. She would claim how she didn't want to hear all of that nonsense from a friend, niece or whomever. But, there was like a relished glee in her eyes that she was receiving more fodder to spew around. She'd be very attentive and ask tons of questions, the epitome of someone who is definitely not uninterested. Then, she'd have such a great time telling me all about it and

33

how pitiful or stupid they were. She'd say how she wished they'd stop bothering her with their mess, but she didn't want to be unkind.

Nevertheless that was for everyone else. For her own children she had no concept of being there. The first time I remember trying to talk to my mother about some teenaged drama I can't even remember, I was about thirteen. Her response was, "I don't have time for your little teenaged issues. I'm too busy dealing with the girls problems."

The "girls" were her drama filled nieces who were much older than I. I learned that my role was that of listener and sympathizer for her. I had to hear how mean and evil my father was whenever she was angry with him or how much she hated him in that moment if she was really ticked at him. While I still lived at home, I was her personal emotional whipping girl. If I didn't show the proper sympathy and agree with whatever poison she was spewing, I was put on restriction, had to hear how mean I was, how I was ungrateful and didn't appreciate or love her. She seemed to do all she could to make my life miserable. The funny thing was, after she was no longer mad at my father she would continue to torture me for not sympathizing with her. Of course, when I got older and moved out I became an ungrateful, unfeeling, mean spirited, evil bitch when I refused to listen to her whining.

For some reason I could never figure out, I was the only one she did this too. Blake and I had an older sister, Aila. We didn't see her much because she moved away to stay away from the drama of our family. However, when we were all home and our mother tried to complain or cry to my sister, Aila would blow her off. Instead of turning her wrath on Aila, I would get it. I would have to hear all about what an airhead my sister was and how she didn't pay any attention to what she said. If I tried playing the airhead, I would have hell to pay.

34

We clearly didn't live in her world. My mother lived in her own world that she created for the outside world. She could brush us off anytime she wanted, but if we brushed her off it was a crisis of epic proportions. If I, however, had the audacity to brush off her toxic waste she'd resort to emotional blackmail, verbal abuse and try to guilt me into being her idea of a daughter.

Maybe because Blake was a guy she didn't expect it of him. Yet, he saw it too. He had been the one who told me I needed to stop mothering her, and he'd been right. It was killing me. And once I cut those emotionally dependent ties with her, I ended up cutting them with all of my needy friends and relatives who seemed to gravitate to me to lean on. I'd had a hard time ever since with allowing anyone to get too close to me. Anyone wanting to get closer than I wanted tended to be shut out. I knew that at some point I would have to risk letting someone in deeper, but I had fought too long and hard to pull myself from the yawning pit of hell my mother had thrown me in for the last time. Protecting my sanity and my emotional stability had become primary. The deeper someone could hurt me the more distantly they had to be kept at bay. And, I was certain if I let Jordan in he could hurt me very deep. I felt too much for him as it was.

Our father was the opposite. He was just simply emotionally unavailable. He wasn't emotionally demanding nor would he allow anyone to be emotionally demanding or dependent on him. Still, I wouldn't say we had an awful upbringing. There were actually lots of fun good times when mother seemed to be happy. Luckily she was happy most of the time. We had lots of really fun, good times. We knew that surface love and affection was there and that was obviously the best our parents could do. It was just so painfully bad when it was bad. Growing up like this taught my siblings and me not to share our feelings, except with each other, and to never depend on anyone, emotionally or otherwise. Obviously, my emotional walls also had almost everything to do with my decision to not let anything progress between Jordan and myself.

The feelings Jordan evoked in me terrified me. He made me want to share. Letting someone else into your emotional life made you weak. Being dependent in any way made you vulnerable. Perhaps because Blake and I had survived by depending on each other, we were comfortable with that. We knew that we had each other's backs. Aila had her husband and she let us in as much as she was able. But to let someone else in was to open yourself up to emotional betrayal and torture. I was disgusted with myself for how easily I'd let Jordan pull me into his side and comfort me when I was frightened out of my mind over the Kevin incident this afternoon. He made me feel out of control, weak and vulnerable, things I already knew I couldn't afford to be. And, he made me feel these warm, fuzzy, squishy feelings, not to mention the hot and bothered fillings low in my groin. It was, in a word, overwhelming.

Jordan pulled into my driveway, and I pulled myself out of the car feeling that bone deep exhaustion only a day with the Alexanders could bring on.

"I guess I should have asked Logan if I needed to take time off," I said breaking the silence. I tried to infuse a note of lightness in my voice that I did not feel.

Jordan climbed out and gave me a barely there nod but said nothing.

"I know John would let me, but it's rather short notice," I said as Jordan followed me to my door. I opened the door and dropped my keys back in my purse.

36

"Logan's already taken care of that, of course," Jordan answered closing the door behind him. He too seemed to be trying not to stir up the dust of the tension surrounding us.

"Of course."

"You can still go to work," he went on. "We only need you when we are interviewing. We don't need you while we are hunting down leads. It's when we find the leads that we need you. Logan's talked to John."

"Let me guess," I said wryly. "You have some dog about to have puppies or something at the ranch and you just want an on call vet tech?"

Jordan actually smiled reluctantly, "Actually, I think he just said he'd need you for the next week."

"Would you like something to drink?" I asked just as my cell phone rang. I dug it out of my purse and saw that it was Shane. I would have to text him or call him back. I was just about to drop the phone back into my purse when Jordan spoke.

"You should probably answer that," he said evenly. I had the feeling he knew who it was.

"It can wait," I responded casually. His jaw seemed to flex with some fleeting emotion before his unreadable expression returned.

"I'm sure he's worried about you. I'd better head out anyway," he said abruptly and turned on his heels.

"No!" I blurted out before I knew it. I didn't want to be alone. All this time I'd thought Kevin was dead and that was why I was safe. Now I knew he wasn't, and I didn't feel safe at all. My phone stopped ringing and Jordan was looking at me intently. "I, uh, wanted to ask you about Kevin."

Understanding crossed his face just as my phone began to ring again. He raised a brow and looked pointedly at the phone. "I think you'd better get that. I'll get a glass of water while you answer that. When you're done, I'll answer whatever questions you have about Kevin."

I nodded and answered the phone.

"Hello?"

"Lela," came Shane's relieved voice. "Is everything ok? You didn't call me."

"I literally just walked in the door. I didn't forget to call you. I just haven't had a chance. But, don't worry. Everything is fine."

"What was that all about?" Shane asked, not sounding convinced.

"Logan wants me to consult on a case, that's all. Nothing to worry about," I reassured him.

"It must be some case. But, that wasn't what I was asking about. I want to know about Jordan?"

"What about him?" I asked cautiously. No doubt Jordan could hear both sides of this conversation with his super human hearing ability.

"Well it was pretty obvious he was angry about finding us together. I just can't figure out if it's because there *was* something going on between the two of you, or there still is."

Well, he certainly wasn't beating around the bush. That was one of the things I liked about Shane usually. He was an upfront, standup sort of guy. Only, I didn't really want to deal with that right now.

"Lela?" Shane's voice sounded in my ear. He wanted answers and I didn't blame him.

"I'm here."

"Are you and Jordan together or involved?"

Yep. Good old blunt Shane.

"Not exactly," I said weakly. In truth we were not together but, our feelings for each other, and our past shared kisses, made saying no feel like a lie. There was definitely something that went on between us.

"Not exactly," he echoed without inflexion. "What *exactly* does that mean?"

"It means no we aren't together, but I can't say there is nothing between us," I began to explain. Who was I kidding? I couldn't do this now.

"Can we talk about this tomorrow? I'm really exhausted," I rushed on. "I promise we'll talk about it tomorrow."

"Tomorrow then," he said after a long pause. He clearly didn't like my answer. "Sleep well, Lela."

"Goodnight," I said quickly and disconnected the phone. I headed into the kitchen where I found Jordan flipping through a spice catalog with a glass of ice water in his hand. He didn't look up when I came in the room.

"So, what did you want to know about Kevin?" he asked distractedly, flipping the page. I didn't believe for a moment that he was that interested in spices. He was still pissed or pissed all over again. As much as that made me want him to leave, I wasn't an idiot. I wanted to know Kevin's minions couldn't get to me.

"Well, now that I know he is still alive. I don't feel quite so safe," I began.

"You want me to kill him?" he asked looking up now at me as if he wasn't necessarily averse to the idea.

"No, of course not," I said calmly. I assumed he was at least half kidding. "I just don't understand why he's not a threat to me."

"He's locked up."

"Yes, but, what if he sends someone else after me? He's got a whole organization of thugs he could send after me. He doesn't work alone."

"Well, from what we've been able to discover, he didn't want you to be able to lead us back to someone else. And, we're under the impression that he really isn't the supreme leader of this group. Logan thinks his job was to keep us off the trail of the organization, specifically someone higher than him in the organization, which is why he came looking for work at the ranch. You were the only one who would possibly be able to identify the two men in the woods, who were apparently two of his men. Once we got to them, they would lead directly to him. And apparently, they assumed that you'd seen more than you had. There were more of them in the woods that day. They had a small camp area about a half mile from where you saw Ethan get shot. They'd been holding him in an old cabin there. They'd had to hastily scrap the camp. But, after they suspected that Ethan was one of us, which was a huge security breach, they suspected you'd been sent there after Ethan and weren't sure how much intel you'd gathered."

"Wouldn't that mean I'm in even more danger?"

"You aren't in any danger, Lela," he stated succinctly. "Ever since Kevin was taken into custody, no one has tried to come near you."

"How do you know that?"

"Because we never removed your security detail," he sighed. "Logan will probably chew my ass for telling you."

"Well, that makes me feel so relieved I can't even be upset about it," I stated, letting out a breath and flopping down into a chair at the kitchen table. "How about we keep it our little secret? Logan doesn't need to know that I know."

40

I grinned at him tentatively, trying to ignore the undesirable response I had to just his proximity. He didn't exactly grin back but his lip twitched.

My body stood at high alert whenever Jordan was near me, and this was no exception. Now that I realized Kevin couldn't just send someone to snuff me out, a familiar ache began low in my belly. No one had ever affected me this way before. It made no sense. The few times he'd kissed me, I'd melted into him without one thought entering my brain as to whether or not this was a good idea. I'd been too busy kissing him back. My physical and jumbled emotional response to him overpowered any rational thoughts. Thankfully we'd been interrupted each time he kissed me, because I honestly wasn't sure if I'd have ever come to my senses and stopped him from taking things all the way. That was a scary thought. I had never been an out of control, hormonal teenager so, I certainly didn't want to start acting like one now that I was a grown woman. And, more importantly, I didn't want my body to write checks that my heart and mind couldn't cash. There were just too many complexities to this me and Jordan idea. He could physically crush me like a bug and do major emotional damage if I let him in. I couldn't afford to take the risks. How I was going to survive working with him remained to be seen.

"Sounds good to me," he said, watching me intently. I got the feeling he was reading something of what I was thinking in my face. I banished all the longing thoughts and concerns and tried for a light, friendly expression.

"So, you, Daisy, and Ethan have been taking turns keeping me safe behind my back?" I said feeling encouraged by his lip twitch. I really did want us to be able to be friends, or at the very least, friendly. "I take it you were here at night since I never saw you."

41

"Something like that."

"So why did you guys keep the security detail on me if Kevin is in custody and no one has come near me?"

"Because we want to make sure that no one comes near you. We don't understand all that is happening yet. And, until we can determine that there is no possibility of a threat, then we have to keep you safe," he stated matter of factly, as if responding to a simple question and answer session with a stranger.

"So is this your normal shift tonight? Because, if it is, you are welcome to stay inside," I offered, continuing my efforts at peacemaking.

"What makes you think I've been spending my nights watching over you outside?" he asked speculatively. He was teasing right? Considering he and the others had the access codes of my security system, and locks weren't a deterrent, he probably wasn't. They all probably came and went as they pleased.

"Thank you. I'd love to stay inside tonight," he said before I was able to formulate a response to his question.

"Make yourself at home. Mi casa es su casa. I'm going to take a shower and go to bed," I said needing to get some sleep. I was too tired to deal with Jordan. I needed to be firing on all cylinders when tangling with him and all his broody male attractiveness.

"Good night," he said reluctantly, as if he wanted to say something. I turned and walked to the door and then remembered I wasn't sure what I was to do tomorrow. Did I go to work or to the ranch?

"Oh, so am I supposed to go to work tomorrow or to the ranch?"

"That's up to you. John knows that Logan contacted you and filled you in. He told Logan you make your own schedule and would work it out."

This was true. I did make my own schedule, but I usually didn't schedule myself offsite for several days at a time. And, I always emailed John my schedule by Friday. So, the one I mailed Friday was now obsolete. As Director of Operations I went wherever I was needed within the business. And, when someone was needed offsite, I would usually schedule one of the vet staff, not myself, to go. Still, technically I was in charge of the Alexander account. So, if they needed something, John would expect me to take care of it as I would any other one of my duties. And, he knew that Logan wanted me specifically and not one of the staff. Logan's call was simply a courtesy call.

"So, if I'm needed tomorrow, then I guess someone will call me?"

"Yes. Just know we may need you. If you do go in to work, don't get into anything you can't be pulled away from at any time."

With that I headed to my room and prepared for bed. Once in bed I called my brother, Blake, to say goodnight. Blake travelled a lot for work and was rarely home. Still, we tried to talk at least once a day. We sort of lived together. Only, he was so rarely home, I felt more like I lived alone in his house and he just came to visit.

"Hey, Baby Girl," he said in greeting. "I called you earlier. Guess you were out with Daisy and Ethan."

"Actually, I was." Well, I was. It wasn't a lie. We just were out working this time.

"Good. I feel better since you've been hanging around them. You spend too much time alone."

"Look who's talking," I said, sounding exasperated.

"Hey, we're not talking about me. We're talking about you. I'm the big brother here," he teased.

43

"Where exactly are you right now?" I asked, brushing off his teasing.

"I'm in New Jersey. But, I'll be home by Friday."

"Really?" I squealed. I missed my brother when he was gone.

"Yes. And, you and I are going to sit down and plan that vacation we were talking about when I get home," he said sternly. "We both have the time since we never use vacation time. So, start thinking of some places you want to go and don't give me any lip. I'll drag you kicking and screaming if I have to."

"I am ready for a vacation," I laughed. "There will be no dragging, kicking, or screaming. I want to relax. I'm thinking of a cruise."

"Mmm, a cruise, huh?" he said mulling it over. "That does sound like a good idea. Where to?"

"Well, I really want to do the Mediterranean. And, I never want to go from country to country in Europe again by train. I think I'm getting too old for that."

"Lela, you're only 22," he said dryly.

"Yea, well, whatever. Anyway, either that or an all-inclusive resort in Costa Rica."

"That sounds good too actually," Blake mused. "So far, I'm liking both. Let me know what you decide and then we can book it."

"You mean *I* can book it," I corrected.

"Yes, that's what I said," he chuckled.

"Whatever, Butt Face," I snorted, calling him by the name I used as a child when he wouldn't give me my way. "Just make sure you leave me your credit card for the booking. Just count my reservations as my booking fee."

"You are such a brat, you know that?" he said with mock annoyance.

"Yea, but you love me. So, it's ok."

He laughed.

"Get some sleep. I'll talk to you tomorrow."

"You too," he said laughing and hung up.

Chapter 7

Around 11:45 Monday Morning, I was sitting at my desk looking over the schedule to determine what things I should delegate so operations wouldn't be interrupted if I were called away, when my phone beeped. It was a text from Ethan.

Call me when you're free. Need to meet with you.

I hit the call back option and Ethan picked up on the first ring. "Hey there gorgeous. Miss me?"

"Of course. Always. I spend every waking moment pining for you," I teased back in the most bored voice I could muster.

"Could you put a little more effort into it? You're really hard on my ego," he retorted in a mock pained voice.

"I'm at the top of my game here, Lover boy. This is the best I can do on short notice," I snorted. "So what's up?"

"Well, I was going to suggest that we meet at about one o'clock for a steamy, hot assignation. But, since you've killed the mood, maybe we can just meet for lunch so I can fill you in on what's going on."

"One o'clock sounds fine," I chuckled.

Both Ethan and Daisy arrived to take me to lunch. We went a couple of blocks over to one of my favorite fast casual restaurants to get a quick Mexican meal. I ordered their Mexican style salad, my personal favorite, while Ethan and Daisy ordered tons of food.

"So, what's happened?" I asked once we were all seated with our food.

"Well, Logan received a call this morning from one of the techs viewing the surveillance at the Beck home. Apparently they picked up something. We weren't sure if they would be able to clean it up enough to get a clear enough picture. Luckily, Logan called just as we got here to pick you up and said it was a go. We need you to be there when we present it to Kevin to see what you can get."

"Ok. When do we go?"

"Logan's setting things up. We have enough time to eat. Then we should be ready to rock," Ethan said digging into his food with gusto.

"I've got some clothes for you to change into," Daisy said also eating with relish. I'd forgotten how much food they could put away. I, on the other hand, had lost my appetite at the idea of having to be near Kevin again. I wasn't quite as fearful as I had been when I'd first found out about Kevin, but it still was nerve racking. I forked up some salad and put it in my mouth. It felt like it was growing larger in my mouth and harder to chew. I focused on chewing it up and swallowing. Both Ethan and Daisy were done in record time. I refrained from putting anything more into my mouth.

Daisy reached out and touched my hand. "Are you ok?"

"I'm fine. I just think I'd rather eat after round two of interrogations."

She gave my hand a sympathetic squeeze, and I took my food to go.

46

Jordan met us at the facility where Kevin was being held. Just like before, Daisy and Jordan stayed in the room with me and I sat against the wall next to the glass. I was thankful that I didn't feel that mind gripping fear I'd had before. It probably proved I was a bit crazy, but my fear was well tempered by anticipation and a growing, exciting fascination. I wondered what I would get this time. I'd always loved a good puzzle. There was a certain pleasure and excitement in knowing that the information I could possibly provide could actually help solve this puzzle. What made the situation even headier was knowing that what I discovered could make the difference in saving a life and preventing further harm. Flooding my mind with these thoughts helped keep the fear away, or at least to a minimum.

Of course, it also meant that what I didn't glean could cost lives or not prevent harm. That pressure was enough to help me keep my fear well contained and my focus on getting everything I could.

Again, I felt Kevin enter the room followed by Logan and Ethan. Jordan automatically handed me pen and paper. Kevin was not feeling so confused now. He was more wary, wondering what exactly Ethan and Logan wanted to know. He was curious for more information also. I scribbled all of the different things I could pick up in my nonsensical scribble. Just as before, Logan kept the interview thankfully short and I was quickly whisked away back to the ranch. Once everyone was seated in the ranch conference room, I began to tell them what I'd found.

"Kevin was wary when he was first brought to the interrogation room, but also curious. He not only wanted to know about why you were interrogating him again, but what your questions could reveal. I got the impression that he has his own suspicions about what happened. And, though he claimed to have never seen the man in the picture before, there was a definite flash of recognition when you showed him the picture," I reported. "I didn't see Kevin's reaction, but when Logan explained that you had reason to believe he knew more than he was telling and asked him if the person in the photo was familiar, I felt a jolt of recognition and strong suspicion from him. It was as though the photo had confirmed something for him. I couldn't tell what exactly. I was hoping maybe you guys were picking up on some facial or body language that revealed more."

"I thought there might be something, but Kevin is really good," Logan said looking thoughtful. "He doesn't give away much. He just stays so calm and cool. Even when we pick up something, we're not sure what it is. So this definitely helps."

"It may sound strange, but I have the same problem. His mind is very controlled. He doesn't do a lot of thinking in words or with clear feelings. I can only pick up what he's thinking or feeling and he really tries to not react, think or feel anything. Most of what I get is fragmented."

"The picture wasn't all that clear," Ethan stated doubtfully. "Are you sure it was recognition."

"Yes. Now what exactly about it he recognized, I don't know. I can only read what he was actually thinking or feeling. Not only did he recognize the person in the photo, but it was also as though it confirmed something for him. Like maybe the person in the picture clarified which of his suspicions were off base and which ones were not. He felt very sure of the person in the picture. To be that sure on an unclear photo, it had to be someone he could recognize just from general physical appearance. Someone he knew well. That is what I felt. Still, it seemed confirming the person in the photo led to more confusion. I don't know if I'm explaining this right," I grumbled in frustration. I tried again. "He definitely knew who was in the picture. However, the confirmation just seemed to cause more confusion. He was giving off a lot of confusion. It seemed to focus his suspicions though, like he knew the person in the picture and that someone was betraying him but he didn't know why? Does that make sense?"

I'd begun to feel like I was babbling. Kevin had so many mixed reactions that they all seemed to contradict each other and I wasn't doing a good job of explaining.

"I am actually following you, I think," Logan said.

"I mean he wasn't actually thinking a lot of words," I continued. "I was picking up all of these feelings and this is what they seemed to reveal to me. Of course, I'm trying to make sense of it without words, but I'm pretty sure this is what it means. The picture created as many questions as it answered and caused just as much confusion as clarity."

The door opened at that point and Ricky and Beto walked in. I hadn't seen them in a while and was momentarily confused. They were the ranch hands I'd spent time with when I worked here at the ranch while the Alexanders tried to figure out who was trying to kill me a little over six weeks ago.

"Hey, Lela. Long time no see," Beto smiled.

"Yea, she must have gotten tired of slumming it with the ranch hands and went back to her nice office job," Ricky said pretending to be insulted.

While I stood there with my mouth open looking confused, Logan spoke into my head.

"Lela, do you mind if we fill Ricky and Beto in on your gift and how you're helping us? They are trusted members of our staff, however, we want to respect your privacy and not reveal it to anyone you don't wish to know."

When I hesitated he went on, not waiting for my reply.

"Think about it. They don't know why you are here and won't ask. They are used to us bringing people in for different reasons. They will only focus on their own tasks and not wonder over much why you are here."

"Did you guys get something new?" Logan asked aloud, turning to Ricky and Beto.

"As a matter of fact we did," Ricky said triumphantly, and started handing out a piece of paper which looked like a sketch. "Shortly after you left, Kevin decided he actually did have some information for us. He called for a guard to give a message to us."

"Really?" Daisy asked skeptically.

"Yea. We thought it was a little suspect as well. Kevin gave the staff the names of two people that might be involved. He even met with a sketch artist and gave descriptions, yet still claims he knows nothing about it," Beto said.

"If he knows nothing about it then how could he possibly offer up suspects?" Ethan snorted.

"That was our question," Ricky picked up the telling. "According to the staff at the holding facility, Kevin says he knows nothing about it but *thinks* he recognizes the person in the picture. He says, if it's who he thinks it is, these other two people would also be involved."

"Did he offer any information on where to find any of them?" Logan questioned.

"Nope. Says he has no idea where they would be. He claims to not know them or their operation well. He just knows who they are."

"It sounds like he's indicating that they are part of a separate organization than his," Logan murmured thoughtfully.

"I'm not sure I believe that though. We have no indication we are dealing with a separate organization and the crime fits his organizations usual activity," Ethan added frowning.

"Ok, you guys head out to the locations we know about and see if we can get eyes on anyone that fits the description of these sketches," Logan commanded. "We'll also put together another team to go out and see if we can find anyone who can identify these guys. Let me know the moment you know something."

"Will do, Boss," Ricky said and headed for the door with Beto on his heels.

Logan called an end to the meeting, or at least my involvement, so that they could decide how to proceed with the new information. I was offered food, but I still had my lunch to eat. So, Jordan hustled me into the car to take me home.

Chapter 8

He was quiet on the way home and kept giving me sidelong glances.

"What, Jordan?" I turned to look at him.

"Nothing," he said thoughtfully sounding as though he were trying to figure something out.

"Then why do you keep sneaking glances at me?" I asked, biting each word out slowly. He was starting to annoy me.

"I just noticed that you don't seem as afraid or upset as you were yesterday. I guess I'm relieved."

"So am I," I smiled, relaxing now.

"I'm wondering why but didn't want to ask, just in case my asking somehow brought on the fear."

I gave a snort of laughter at that. Of course I still had a healthy dose of fear, but I wasn't scared shitless like I'd been yesterday. "Well, you don't have to worry. I'm not likely to be gripped with fear at the power of your suggestion."

"I'm more relieved than you know…I think. But, why aren't you afraid or upset about being so close to Kevin?"

"Oh, I am still afraid. I couldn't even eat my lunch," I assured him. "The biggest relief was that I didn't get the impression that he knew I was there today or yesterday."

"Well, that's good to know," he replied sounding genuinely relieved. "Uh, how exactly do you know this?"

"Well, I can't say that I am certain, but he never had a thought about me. I realized that I never got any impression that he recognized me through the glass yesterday. I don't believe something wouldn't have at least skittered across his mind if he had known I was there."

"Then why did he smile at you at the first interrogation?"

I shuddered at the memory, "To rile whomever was behind the glass like Daisy said. He likely saw our silhouettes standing there. If I'd not reacted and just paid attention to what I was picking up, I would have realized sooner that he didn't show any recognition, just arrogance and bluster."

"Well, I'm sure everyone will be relieved to hear that. So, what's the other reason you are so at ease with all this today?"

I shrugged my shoulders together and couldn't help the huge smile that crossed my face. "I'm finding it quite intriguing actually. It's like a very important puzzle that I get to help solve."

"Ah, I see," Jordan glanced at me and returned my smile politely.

"I don't know how to explain it," I said as he pulled into my driveway. I opened my door and slid out just as he stepped out of the driver's side. "It still scares me down to my toes, but the idea that I can really help save a life or solve this puzzle is, well, intriguing."

"I can understand that," Jordan said as I opened the door. "I often feel that way myself. It's a very satisfying feeling."

"It is. So, are you burdened with the duty of my protection tonight again?"

"I am. And it's not a burden."

"It's a little early. What do you want to do?" I asked, dropping my keys in my purse and dropping my purse by the door.

"Doesn't matter to me. My job is to protect you. So, whatever you decide to do I just have to go along with it." He sounded almost bored. This distant and blank attitude towards me was starting to grate on my already frayed nerves.

"Really? So if I want to go for a run, you have to go with me?" I teased, trying to lighten him up a bit. I turned to look at him with my arms crossed.

"Yes, but I'd suggest an elliptical or treadmill since you can't keep up with me running."

Was he teasing back? Not likely. The look on his face leaned more towards just stating a fact.

"Hey," I said poking him in the chest. He captured my hand and held it as he looked down at me. His eyes softened and just like that my heart started racing and my belly did strange things. "You don't look irritated."

"Am I supposed to be?"

"Yes. Being poked is supposed to be irritating," I grumbled looking up into his lovely, fathomless eyes. He had such nice eyes. They were a deep, muddy sea green sometimes depending on the lighting. However, when the light hit them just right, I could see gold flecks. And, when he smiled his whole face lit up and made me feel all warm and fuzzy inside. As I stood there gazing into his handsome face, I realized that he was gazing into mine.

"It's very hard for me to remember that you're only interested in being friends when you look at me like that," he said in a low, husky tone.

"I'm sorry," I said, my voice sounding breathy, and I looked away. He didn't release my hand, and I could feel him looking at me and waiting. Stop being a coward, I told myself. I looked up to meet his eyes again.

"I'm really trying, Lela, even though I know you are just as attracted to me as I am to you. Still, I'm trying to give you what you want."

"Why?" I wasn't sure I intended to ask the question, but I didn't understand why he bothered with me at all. It was clear that rejecting his feelings for me was frustrating for him.

He frowned. "Why am I trying to be your friend?"

"Well, yes."

"Because I *am* your friend. I care for you. And, whether we are lovers or not doesn't change the fact that I care for you, not just as a lover but as a person." There was a sweet dip in my nether regions when he said the word lover. How stupid was that?

He cupped my chin and brushed his thumb lightly along my cheek. "I don't want to not have you as a friend just because I want to be more than that. Only, I don't know how to be just your friend, either."

My cell phone chirped causing me to jump. Jordan dropped his hand from my face and stepped back. I turned quickly to my purse and began digging through it to get to my phone. I needed to break this connection that always seemed to flow between us when we were together. I dug the phone out, glanced at the screen, saw it was Shane and decided I couldn't answer it now. I needed to talk to Shane, but I couldn't do it with Jordan around. Jordan glanced at it too.

"You can answer it you know. I'll go in the other room or outside if you want privacy." His eyes had hardened again.

"No, I can talk to him later."

He watched me quietly for a moment as the phone continued to ring. I placed the phone on the mail table and turned to grab the mail. One piece of mail caught my eye and I hesitated. Anger filled me and I ripped up the envelope, walked over to the trash and dumped it in.

"I think I want to go for a swim," I said when the phone finally went to voicemail.

"So we aren't going to talk about this?"

I looked at him and he gave me a pointed look. Only, now he was looking confused. Was he going to ask me about the envelope now too?

"What do you want me to say, Jordan?" I pleaded not wanting to talk anymore. I was starting to feel like I was being caved in on all sides.

"If I had kissed you before your phone rang you wouldn't have stopped me. I want to know how you can keep denying what's between us," he gritted out. Then he took a deep breath and the next words came out in a whisper. "And, I want to know if you're sleeping with Shane."

I blinked in surprise. I certainly hadn't been expecting that. I wanted to tell him that it was none of his business, however, even I was too chicken to utter those words with him glaring down on me like an angry Zeus getting ready to shoot lightning bolts at me with his eyes. I must have stood there staring with my mouth open a moment too long, because Jordan's eyes got all flinty again as if he were ready to shoot fire from them.

"Damn you, Lela," he growled at me. He was standing rigid clenching and unclenching his fists at his side. Clearly he'd taken my silence as confirmation.

"Leave, Jordan," I bit out through clenched teeth in my own rush of anger. How could he think such a thing of me? And, even if I had, it wasn't like we were together. He had no right. So much for being friends. I refused to let Jordan send me spiraling and I had reached my limit of emotional calm.

"I'm not going anywhere until you tell me why," he growled, stepping quickly forward causing me to step back until there was nothing but a wall behind me. "Why is it that you fight your attraction to me, what we could have together, but fall into bed with someone else?"

I raised my chin and stared at him defiantly as I shook all over. Strangely, I wasn't afraid he would hurt me. But, having all his burning rage directed at me still made me shake. Maybe my body's reaction was smarter than my brain's. He closed his eyes, placed a hand on the wall on each side of my head and dropped his head down to his chest as if pulling deep for calm and patience. When he glanced up at me moments later, the burning rage was now burning pain in his eyes. It was my undoing.

"I just want to understand why, Lela," he said gruffly but calmly. "Can you at least tell me that? And, don't give me the part about not being safe with me. We both know I would never hurt you."

"I didn't fall into bed with anyone, Jordan." My voice didn't come out quite as scathing as I'd meant it to be. "How can you just assume that of me? Not that it would have been any of your business if I had."

56

Now it was his turn to stare mutely at me, quiet relief slowly seeping into his eyes.

"Do you want him, Lela?"

"No," I sighed. Though I'd thoroughly enjoyed Shane's kiss, he was an excellent kisser, I didn't want him.

We just stood there looking at each other, our faces so close our breath mingled. Then, he was leaning towards me and I was leaning towards him. His mouth gently covered mine and he pulled me closer with one hand around my waist. And, as usual, with no connection between my brain and my bodily response, I melted into him as if the six weeks apart had never happened. The kiss was sweet and light and full of tenderness. Finally, some part of my brain that was trying to be heard had me pulling away.

"You want me, Lela," he murmured against my mouth, "just as much as I want you. I can tell by the way you kiss me."

I dropped my hands. Somehow they'd fisted in his shirt of their own accord. "Jordan, I –"

"No, Lela," he cut me off. "Don't pull away from me. I get that you are afraid or whatever. We'll go slowly. But, stop running away from me."

Even as my brain was yelling, 'No! Don't do it!' my heart was saying yes...as was my body.

"Say it, Lela. Stop fighting and say it," he commanded and then pressed his lips to mine for a long, slow, persuasive kiss.

"Ok, Jordan. Ok." It sounded like a whimper, even to my own ears. He looked at me now and a slow, triumphant smile spread across his face. Then he pulled me to him and kissed me senseless.

"I really need to swim now," I breathed once he released me. I was going to try. Yes, I was very apprehensive of the unknown, but I didn't

57

want to fight this anymore. Still, I felt like I was in a panic. My skin felt all tingly and tight. I thought about the ripped up envelope in the trash and tried to ignore my mind screaming at me to not let anyone else in. Letting people get close to you was a sure way to open yourself up to hurt. I beat back my growing hysteria and tried to appear calm and sane when I spoke again. "Care to join me?"

"Sure," Jordan said looking at me with a hint of puzzlement and caution in his eyes. "Let me get my gym bag out of the car. I'll change and meet you poolside."

Chapter 9

Five minutes later we were swimming laps back and forth across the pool. I was swimming hard to burn off some of the excess energy I felt. Usually, a good hard workout helped me beat my mind back into submission when it threatened to take over and paralyze me with overwhelming emotions.

Despite my manic swimming, Jordan made me look like I was standing still, the showoff. After almost twenty minutes I stopped to catch my breath. Jordan was still going as if he was on his first few laps. I waited until he reached my side of the pool and completed his flip turn, and I pounced on his legs and held on for dear life. He immediately stopped and jerked around to see what I was doing, which sent me flying as I let go.

"What are you doing?" he sputtered as I surfaced a few feet away and began splashing him in the face with water. Knowing he could drown me with the water he'd send my way if he returned my water splashes, I dove under and swam towards the side of the pool. I'd barely gotten two strokes in when he had me by the ankle. I put my other foot down and hopped on one leg as he gently pulled me towards him.

"Do you really want to have a water war with me?" he asked looking puzzled but smiling.

"No. I just wanted to slow you down since you were being such a show off," I laughed still hopping on one leg. "Now, let my leg go."

"Show off? What are you talking about?" He didn't release my leg. I tried to jerk it out of his grasp, slipped on my hopping foot and went under. I was still laughing when I went under and ended up swallowing a mouthful of water. Jordan grabbed me by the waist before I could get my footing and pulled me up sputtering and coughing.

"Stop laughing and breath, silly woman," he said with amusement. "What is so funny anyway?"

"The look of surprise on your face when I grabbed your legs," I said coughing into his chest. When he'd grabbed me, I'd reached out reflexively and grabbed his arms. He'd pulled me up and against his chest. As my coughing subsided, I was rapidly becoming aware of being in his arms. I looked up to see him looking down at me with confused amusement dancing in those mossy green eyes.

"I was just thinking about how I was swimming so hard and you looked like you weren't even making any effort, yet you were lapping me like I was the one not making any effort," I began babbling. Jordan's smile faded and his face took on a more serious look as his eyes turned heated. I stopped talking. How could I continue to fight this when being in his arms felt so good, so safe, so right?

Jordan squeezed his eyes closed and tightened his grip around my waist. I couldn't move. I just watched the play of emotions crossing his clenched face.

"Tell me to let you go," he breathed out between his pursed lips. With eyes still closed, he took in another deep breath, brought his forehead to mine, and let out a long breath.

I stood there in his arms, reveling in the feel of him. I couldn't have spoken the words if I'd wanted to. Being in his arms had done more to pull me back from my emotional edge than all of the swimming I'd been doing. He opened his eyes and looked into mine and heat flooded all through my body.

"Ah, hell," he mumbled before lowering his head and bringing his lips down on mine. Unable, and admittedly unwilling, to fight this need for him anymore, I gave in to the kiss. Feeling my body yielding into his, he released my waist with his right hand and placed it behind my head while he pulled me tighter against him. I willingly opened my mouth to his probing tongue and he fisted his hand in my hair as he deepened the kiss. This kiss was proving to be more devastating than the last one. Before today, it had been over six weeks since I'd kissed Jordan and the effort I'd expended denying our attraction had only made me weaker in his arms. Though he said we would take things slow, he seemed to be making up for lost time today in the kissing department and I was helpless to resist.

Desire burned through me unchecked and even as my mind warned me to slow down and stay in control I was burning out of control. I had no more will power left when it came to this man and that scared the hell out of me. But, even that feeling of being recklessly out of control wasn't enough for me to regain some semblance of control now. I was caught up in the feelings he evoked and nothing else existed but the assault of sensation after sensation he was bombarding me with. Even the roiling emotions the torn up envelope caused were pushed back into the far reaches where they belonged.

60

After some time, Jordan slowly began to loosen his grip on my hair and around my waist. His kiss became gentle and heartbreakingly sweet before he finally lifted his head, breaking the kiss. As reality came back to me, I could hear a ringing sound. A phone was ringing. I hadn't heard it until Jordan released me from his spell. He looked at me as if trying to read something in my face for a long moment. Our harsh breathing and that damn phone were the only sounds.

"I'd better get that," he said finally with a slight grin on his face.

"Yea, ok." I replied dumbly. He released me, hopped out of the pool in one fluid motion and walked over to the patio table where his phone sat.

"Hey, Daisy, what's up?"

"I just wanted to make sure Lela was with you. She's not answering her phone," Daisy's voice came over the phone speaker.

"Yea, she's with me. Her phone is inside and we were swimming outside."

Daisy hesitated a long moment before she finally spoke, "Oh, good. Well, I was planning on coming over tonight if that's alright?"

"Of course, it's alright," I called out loud enough to be heard by Jordan's phone speaker. I hoped she would assume my heavier than normal breathing was due to swimming. I could almost hear Daisy's wheels turning. Daisy knew my reasons for not wanting to get involved with Jordan, and I knew she was hoping I would get over them. She didn't interfere…much, but I knew she thought I was right for her brother – in – law and he was right for me.

"Well, if you're sure?" came her disembodied voice. "I mean, I was just thinking we could hang out, but we don't have to."

"Daisy, it's totally fine," I assured her. "If nothing comes up with the case, we can catch up on some of our shows on the DVR."

"Ok, then. I'm on my way."

I hopped out and began to towel myself off. Jordan sighed in seeming frustration, ran a hand through his wet hair and sighed. "I blew it again, didn't I?"

"Why do you say that?" I asked, toweling off my dripping hair and enjoying the view of Jordan in nothing but his swim jammers.

"I'm supposed to be keeping my hands off of you and the first chance I get, they're all over you again."

The very idea of Jordan with his hands all over me was cause for spontaneous combustion. I very rigidly beat my libido back into submission. While, I was beginning to realize that fighting this attraction between us was a lost cause, that didn't mean I had to jump in head first. Taking things slowly would still be the wiser course of action.

"I can't see how it could be all your fault. It wasn't as though I was fighting you off."

"Sooo, what are you saying?" Jordan asked slowly, his lust darkened eyes watching me with laser focus now.

"I'm just saying that it's hardly all your fault when I seem to be a willing participant each time our lips seem to get stuck together."

"Is this where you're going to start pulling away from me and rebuilding your walls to keep me out?" He asked cautiously.

I let out a humorless snort, "Apparently, that's not very effective. And, I don't think I have the energy to keep shoring them up. You just break them down again."

Jordan was quiet. I stopped drying my hair and looked over at him. He had a quizzical look I was beginning to realize he often wore around me. Poor guy. I must confuse him as much as I confused myself.

"What about Shane?"

"What about him?"

"Well, the idea of sharing you with him doesn't appeal to me at all. As a matter of fact, I'm pretty sure I couldn't do it. And, since I walked in on you kissing him just a couple of days ago, I think I have a right to know just how involved with him you are. I didn't see you putting up any resistance with him either."

I winced. He had a point. As much as I wanted to pretend that it never happened, I felt the need to explain myself. I wasn't the type of girl that just went around kissing different guys.

"Shane and I aren't really involved," I said, beginning my awkward explanation. "That kiss sort of just happened."

"Just happen? So, that kiss wasn't headed to the bedroom?"

"No!" I looked directly into his eyes feeling myself flushing with embarrassment, but determined to make it clear. "Jordan, that was the first time I'd even kissed him, or rather he kissed me."

"Oh," he replied visibly relaxing. A grin was tugging at the corners of his mouth trying to break free. "That's good to know."

"I've only known him for roughly six weeks, Jordan."

He shrugged as if that really didn't mean much but didn't say anything. And, well I guess it probably didn't. I wasn't sure what the average time was for people to start hitting the sheets but six weeks was probably enough time for lots of people. I started to ask him, if I hadn't slept with him in less than 6 weeks of knowing him then why would he even imagine I'd have slept with Shane? But, on second thought, it seemed better to abandon this whole line of conversation.

"I'm going to take a shower before Daisy gets here. I'm starving since I still haven't eaten my lunch, but I need to get cleaned up first. You can use the hall bathroom," I threw over my shoulder as I grabbed my towel and headed inside.

Chapter 10

Daisy arrived just as I was coming out of my room freshly showered and in a pair of Blake's shorts. There was nothing more comfortable then wearing my brother's oversized shorts and sweats to lounge around in, though, Blake would probably argue the point.

We spent the evening catching up on the shows I'd recorded on the DVR. Ethan arrived shortly after Daisy. It was like any other random evening except for Jordan's presence. When I'd been originally put under the protection of the Alexanders, Ethan, Daisy and I had spent many an evening watching the DVR. Ethan would often cook or we'd get take out. Tonight they decided on take out. As soon as Ethan and Jordan left to pick up the food, Daisy pounced on the opportunity to drill me.

"So, it looks like you and Jordan are better now," she stated.

"Jordan and I are fine," I said giving her a warning look.

"What about the delectable, Shane?" She asked mischievously.

"What about him?"

"Oh, come on, Lela. Do tell," she whined. "That kiss looked pretty hot to me, and Jordan was pissed. He wouldn't be here hanging out if you guys didn't work something out. But, where does that leave poor Shane?"

"Seriously, Daisy? It was just a kiss. And, I'm not discussing this with you."

"You have to," her high whine was starting to get on my nerves. "That's what girlfriends do. We talk about guys."

"Well, one of the guys happens to be related to you." I gave her a pointed look.

"True, but I'm not asking about him. Those details you can keep to yourself. Of course, if you two time him, I might have to hurt you really bad. Jordan is the closest thing to a brother I have, well, besides Ethan." She stated matter of factly. "But, you don't strike me as the type. So, if you and Jordan are ok now, what's the harm in giving me details about Shane?"

"Threats now? Charming."

"Oh, you know I wouldn't harm you," she said, waving her hands around impatiently. "What was going on with you and Shane? I have no idea how I missed it."

"The truth?"

"Yes!"

"There was nothing going on between Shane and I. He kissed me and you guys walked in," I shrugged. "End of story."

"Seriously? You guys weren't secretly seeing each other?"

"No. And, if we were, why would we keep it a secret?"

"True," she frowned. "Well, that was anticlimactic."

"So sorry to disappoint," I said with exaggerated cheerfulness.

"Then, if it isn't Shane, what else is bothering you? You are very quiet tonight and somehow it doesn't seem to be because of Jordan."

"What is it with you?" I glared at her. "Why are you psycho-analyzing me?"

"I'm not. I'm just worried about you," she said sounding a little hurt. "You aren't yourself today. You seem very quiet and have disappeared inside yourself. You're more self-possessed than usual and seem to be keeping your mask very carefully in place. It worries me. Sorry. I'll leave you be."

Damn her perceptiveness.

"Daisy, I just don't want to talk about it. Suffice it to say, old ghosts coming back to haunt me, along with the case and Jordan. I just have a lot on my mind," I said tiredly. "I'm fine. Please just let it go."

She nodded and we sat there in an uncomfortable silence.

The guys finally returned with the food, easing the tension in the room. Ethan set about in the kitchen pulling out dishes and setting things up buffet style. Jordan frowned several times at Ethan's familiarity with the kitchen and house but, as Daisy was also just as familiar and comfortable moving about the house, he seemed to realize that he was the only one who hadn't been around enough to be so at home. After filling our plates we sat down in the family room and cued or favorite detective show up on the DVR. Ethan took a seat next to me on the left while Jordan took a seat next to me on the right on the big sofa in the family room. Ethan seemed to do everything he could to try and piss Jordan off. He threw his arm around me and pulled me into his side, only to have Jordan grab his arm and push it off of me. He tried to play with my hair only to have Jordan punch him in the shoulder. After he bent down to whisper in my ear and Jordan punched him again, I got up and went to sit with Daisy on the loveseat. Neither of them seemed to be mad. It was like watching two teenagers punching and hitting each other and trying to annoy each other. I just refused to be the toy they decided to bicker over for fun.

Chapter 11

The next morning I found myself in my office staring at my phone. I needed to call Shane. He hadn't called me back again. I knew I owed him an explanation, but I just didn't know what to say. After a few more moments of lip biting, I decided I would just tell him the truth. I picked up the phone and dialed.

"Good morning, Lela," came his low silky voice. He sounded cheerful. That was good. "What a pleasant surprise."

"Good morning, Shane," I smiled, feeling relieved that he didn't sound disgruntled or angry.

"For a moment there, I thought you were avoiding me."

"Honestly, I wasn't avoiding you. It's just been a bit hectic. I'm sorry for taking so long to get back to you."

"Not a problem," he answered good naturedly.

"So, about Sunday –"

"From the way Jordan reacted, I think I understand what happened Sunday," he interrupted. "I just wanted to make sure you were alright. Not that I thought he would hurt you, but I didn't want you guys fighting because of me. I should never have kissed you. I wouldn't have if I'd known you and Jordan were involved."

I started to let it go at that but figured that wasn't fair. And, it made me look like I was a cheater. "Actually, Jordan and I weren't involved, not really."

Shane made a non-committal sound.

"What I mean is, I had decided that I didn't want to get involved with Jordan and had told him that. So we weren't actually involved."

"I see. So, there is nothing going on between you two?"

"Well, not exactly. We have unresolved issues. And, until those issues get resolved then I think I'd better not create new issues. I am the one who is sorry. I should have never let you kiss me. I mean I hadn't seen

Jordan in weeks. I don't want you to think I'd do something like that. I wouldn't be kissing you if I was with Jordan."

"Lela, I understand. You don't have to explain things to me. I figured you guys must be working things out when I came by the other night and saw his car in the driveway." His voice was gentle.

"You came by?"

"Like I said, I just wanted to make sure you were ok. I thought you were alone so, I wanted to check on you."

"Oh," was all I could say. Well that was embarrassing. Trying to explain that nothing happened that night would just make me look…, weird. "Look, this thing between Jordan and I is still very new. We haven't worked it out yet."

"Lela, I get it. And I'm not that type of guy who wants to get in-between someone else's relationship. You don't have to explain it to me. I've got the gist. I just hope that Jordan doesn't forbid us from being sparring partners. I don't know Jordan all that well. But, I like the guy. I really like you Lela, but I would never have touched you if I'd known he was interested."

I had nothing to say to that. Logan had been the one to refer Shane to me for martial arts sparring. He had taught me so much through the ass – kickings he'd given me over the last six weeks. Granted he'd never really hurt me or tried to. But, one was bound to acquire a few bumps and bruises when fighting. He'd wanted to make sure I was combat ready, and I definitely was. I still attended the classes I'd been attending before I met the Alexanders, but I'd grown much better through my sparring sessions with Shane. Since I'd never seen him with or around the Alexanders, except for the few times he'd run into Daisy and Ethan at my house, I'd never really thought about how well they knew each other.

"Not that I'm not extremely attracted to you," he said bringing me out of my reverie. "But, if we ever got together, I'd want you free of any other encumbrances. So, friends?"

"Friends," I said feeling relieved. "Thank you, Shane."

"No worries, Babe. We are all good."

After my talk with Shane, I'd spent the rest of the day taking care of various things I hadn't gotten to in the office. I was relieved that our kiss hadn't seemed to make our relationship complicated. Hopefully, sparring wouldn't be awkward.

I caught up on department reports, other paperwork, and even had time to help out in the training building and veterinary clinic. It was almost the end of the day when Daisy called.

"Hey, Daisy. What's happened?"

"Nothing so far. We've had teams trying to identify the people in the sketches that Kevin gave us, but they don't seem to exist. If they do exist, they are very well hidden. Anyway, I'm off duty, so I was going to swing by and hang out. I thought maybe we could stop by the creamery. A hot fudge sundae is calling my name. I was sorta hoping one was calling you too."

"I can meet you there in about 20 minutes," I laughed.

Once we were seated, and our ice cream orders were taken, Daisy got started in on me again. "I know it's none of my business, but I just have to ask. What is going on with you and Jordan now? I've noticed he's been spending nights at your house too. That's two nights in a row."

"What are you talking about?" I frowned. My voice was sarcastic. "One of you guys is always at my house. I know about the security detail. He told me that one of you guys is always at my house at night, even when I don't know it. I thought you were going to fill me in on the case."

"Jordan hasn't been assigned to you in weeks. Then, suddenly he tells Ethan and me that he's taking over night duty at your house." She raised a brow. "Something is going on. And, since we're friends, well, these are the things BFF's tell each other."

"Oh, so we are BFF's now? Yesterday it was girlfriends," I said sardonically. "And, what do you mean Jordan hasn't been assigned to me for weeks. He told me that someone was always at my house in the evenings. I thought you guys rotated?"

"We do rotate. Ethan and me. On those days that I'm not staying over to hang out, Ethan, I, or someone else is there. Someone other than Jordan. Logan thought you'd get cranky about it if you knew. Jordan wasn't supposed to tell you."

"So, all those nights you and Ethan were hanging out with me, you were just protecting me?" Ok, my voice did sound a little strained. Daisy narrowed her eyes at me and started wagging her finger at me.

"Oh, no. Don't even try it. You know that's not true. And we are girlfriends and BFF's. At least, you are my BFF. Ethan and I could have just fallen into regular rotation. We hang out with you because you're one of us. You're our friend. You are more than a friend, you're like my sister. Don't you dare question my friendship," she huffed. "Now, spill it about you and Jordan. What's going on?"

"You spill it about the case," I shot back.

There's nothing going on with the case right now. Nothing new has come up. I already told you, Logan is still working with his intel crew to figure out who these suspects are and following leads. Nothing concrete has been uncovered yet. For the moment, we are on standby. Your turn."

"There's nothing going on with Jordan and me. I just thought he was assigned to night duty. When I asked him about Kevin and how you

70

guys knew there was no threat from him and his organization, he said that the security detail had never been removed. So, I told him that he didn't need to stay outside at night now that I knew about it. And, now that I know Kevin is alive, I certainly won't be upset about being guarded."

"Jordan is totally different and you expect me to believe nothing is going on?" She asked and then changed subjects so fast my head was spinning. "Is Shane a good kisser?"

I sat there blinking at her, trying to keep up with her sporadic topic changes.

I bet that man can kiss," she grinned conspiratorially. "Not that I am rooting for him because really, I think you and Jordan are made for each other. Besides, he's family so I have to be on his side."

"Daisy, you are nuts." I stared at her as if she'd lost her mind.

"All I'm doing is gossiping about your love life. It happens to be far more interesting than mine at the moment." She frowned. "And you are not cooperating at all."

Thankfully our sundaes came and I was able to direct the conversation away from my so called love life. I dug into my sundae. There was nothing like a hot fudge sundae with cake batter and chocolate ice cream to make me feel like a kid inside. I'd have to hit the elliptical when I got home but it was worth it. Just as we were finishing up our sundaes, Daisy's phone rang. She answered and after listening for a moment said goodbye.

"We have to go," she stated, all business now.

"What's going on?"

"The suspect that was on the video, the one we showed Kevin, it turns out he did exist," she said pulling out cash and placing it on the

71

table. I took out enough cash for my sundae and a tip and placed it on the table with hers.

"Are we going to go interview him?" I asked as I stood and gathered my purse.

"No. He was found dead."

Chapter 12

Everyone was already assembled when we got to the ranch. We took our seats and Logan began speaking.

"Good. We are all here. Lela, you won't have to sit in on an interrogation just yet, but I wanted you to be up to speed. Our murdered suspect's name is Jason Walker. It's not a coincidence that we showed this man's picture to Kevin and then he ends up dead. And, when we informed him Mr. Walker was dead, it didn't take a mind reader to see that Kevin wasn't surprised. He must have ordered a hit on him. What we want to find out is how and why. Rene and Maya found out that Kevin has had a few visitors besides us. We suspect they are all part of the organization so we are trying to track them down. We will need you on hand for their interrogations. We hope to round some, if not all of them, up by morning so you might want to get some sleep. And don't plan to go into work in the morning. Sorry for the inconvenience."

"No problem, Logan." I waved away his apology. I was musing over the idea that Maya and Rene were also part of the investigation. I had met them during my first visits here as well, but I hadn't seen them since my case ended.

"You might not feel that way when we are pulling you out of your bed in the middle of the night. But, we have to move as fast as we can. Time is short." Logan's voice was still apologetic yet commanding.

"Strong coffee helps," I teased. He smiled.

Logan gave everyone their orders and dismissed the meeting. Daisy was assigned to take me home and stay with me for the night. Just in case they located someone, Daisy could drive me to wherever they needed me to be. Jordan was assigned to follow leads in an attempt to locate Kevin's visitors. He walked me to Daisy's waiting car.

"I got a call from Shane today." He was smirking, waiting for my surprised reaction when I stopped dead in my tracks and looked at him.

"Why?" I finally stammered.

"He wanted to make sure there were no hard feelings between us. He said he didn't know we were involved, and that I shouldn't be mad at you because the kiss was entirely his doing. He said he caught you off guard."

"Did he now?" I said feeling my eyes narrow. "I wasn't aware you guys knew each other so well."

He just grinned. "I so want to kiss you right now, but Daisy's watching us, the nosey little brat. You'd better go. I'll come by tonight when I'm done."

I turned and saw that Daisy was indeed sitting in the driver seat staring directly at us. I turned back to Jordan and he winked at me and started walking backwards, back towards the house. He waved and I waved back and headed for the car.

Daisy and I spent a quiet evening, watching television. For once she seemed to be the one engrossed in thought and didn't bug me once with personal questions. I thought to ask her what was going on in her head, but decided that she might turn it back on me if I did. Better to just let her brood in peace.

When we still hadn't heard anything by nine in the evening I decided I'd better go to bed. If I stayed up late with Daisy, they'd be waking me up in the middle of the night just as Logan said. I didn't do well on little sleep. So I showered, crawled into bed, and drifted off to sleep.

Several hours later, I was awakened by the sound of Jordan softly calling my name and caressing my face with gentle fingers.

"Lela, wake up, sweetheart."

"Jordan?" I opened my eyes to find Jordan lying next to me, propped up on an elbow and looking down at me. I smiled. "Hey. What time is it?"

"Hey, yourself, and it's three am."

"When did you get here?"

"A few hours ago. I've been sitting here watching you sleep."

"Why?" I frowned.

"I like to watch you sleep."

"You do know that's creepy right?"

He just smiled, then bent down and gave me a quick kiss. "Mmm, I'd better not start that. Sorry, love, but we have to go."

"Go? They found someone?" I yawned and stretched.

"Lela," he said in a husky tone, "don't do that or we are never getting out of this bed."

"Do what?"

"All that yawning and stretching. You're all sexily rumpled and sleepy warmth." He kissed me again, but this time he put an arm under the covers and pulled me to him. I was instantly flooded with heat and need. My arms went around his neck and my whole body was tingling and aware of his partial weight on me as I opened my mouth to him. Who was

74

I kidding? I was his for the taking. While the ease with which he made me feel totally out of control still frightened me, my desire for him was waging its own war against my caution. I felt Jordan smile against my mouth as he eased away and I realized my hands were fisted in his hair.

"Logan will kill me if we don't get moving. But, just know that I'm planning to pick up right here when we're done with these interviews. And don't even think about going all shy on me. You want me Lela Charles, just as much as I want you."

He bent down and nipped my lower lip and then eased off of the bed. "Now get up woman and get dressed. We have work to do."

Chapter 13

As far as I could tell the interrogations were a bust. Three of Kevin's four visitors were found. Aside from the fact that I could confirm two of them were part of Kevin's organization, and that they also knew the now dead man, I didn't get any new information. The third man was just a college student who was just there to do a report for a law class. It was obvious that he was completely confused about why he was being interrogated. He had no idea what was going on. He was a healer who had interviewed Kevin to do a report for another student. His law professor also happened to be one of the attorneys that worked for the facility. While regular humans didn't know who the healers and drainers were living among them, they knew each other. And, those students often were able to do their research on cases involving drainers and healers. Apparently, healers were just as capable of killing as saving and sometimes did, or they committed other crimes just like in any other human population.

The other two of Kevin's visitors were human. They carried out their orders like soldiers. However, they had nothing to do with the killing of Jason Walker. I sensed fear and confusion from them also. Apparently, they weren't sure what happened to Walker and weren't sure if they would be next. They were too busy trying to stay focused on not giving away anything for fear that they would end up just like Walker to be of much help. Something was going on, that was clear to them. But, they didn't know what it was. Their minds were just a jumbled mass of confused fear. The whole thing felt like an exercise in futility.

It was only 11 am Wednesday morning when we arrived back at the ranch, but I felt like I'd been up all day. I was tired and hungry. Logan wanted to keep me around just in case they rounded up Kevin's remaining visitor for questioning.

"Have some breakfast and then you can go up and take a nap in my room if you like," Jordan suggested quietly in my ear.

"Breakfast sounds good, but I think I'd rather use one of the guest rooms for a nap," I whispered back. It just seemed way too presumptuous to make myself comfortable in Jordan's room. Maybe it was my old fashion upbringing, but it just didn't seem right.

"Suit yourself. Just get some food and rest. You didn't get much sleep last night and you're dead on your feet," Jordan sighed.

"You can use one of the guest rooms up the stairs and to the right," Logan said and winked at me. He'd remained silent through the hushed exchange between me and Jordan until now.

"Thanks," I said feeling awkward. I wasn't a prude, but I certainly wasn't as casual as Jordan was about such things. I wouldn't just plop myself down in my not even official boyfriends bed for a nap in his family home. It just wasn't done in my family.

76

We walked into the breakfast room and Grace was sitting at the table with her not quite two year old daughter, Daniela, and three year old son, Tyler. I had only seen the children twice in the whole time I'd known the Alexanders. When I'd worked here, I never saw them during my working hours. I'd only seen them the two times I'd been here at purely social events.

"Uncle Jordan!" Daniela yelled the moment Jordan entered the room. She scrambled down from her chair at the table and ran at him with open arms.

"What about, Daddy?" Logan frowned as Jordan picked up Daniela.

"Uncle Jordan lets us have pastries," Tyler grinned in delight.

"Does he now?" Grace said giving Jordan a stern look as he cradled his niece in his arms.

"Busted," Logan snickered under his breath.

"Hello, Lela," Grace smiled. "Please forgive my rude daughter. Grab a plate and eat. I'm sure you're famished."

"Thanks, Grace."

"You can sit by me," Tyler smiled smacking a hand down on a chair next to him.

"No, she's a girl. She sits with the girls, Tyler," Daniela insisted.

"How about she sits with me and we'll both sit with the both of you," Jordan suggested firmly.

"And I sit on your lap?" Daniela batted her eyes at Jordan as only little girls can.

"Of course you can, pumpkin," Jordan cooed rubbing his nose against hers. She giggled.

"Not while you are eating, young lady," came Grace's stern voice. "You will sit in your chair. Logan make her behave. I have to go. Don't let her get away with that, and don't you guys feed her sweets."

"Yea, because she's a brat," Tyler added with great authority.

"Don't call your sister a brat, Tyler," Grace said turning her stern mommy voice on Tyler. Then she stood and grabbed her own empty plate. Tyler went back to eating his fruit bowl unbothered by his reprimand.

"Go on, Grace. We've got the kids," Logan said taking the empty plate from Grace's hand and bending to give her a kiss. Then Grace was out the door.

I grabbed a plate and put some eggs, sausage, berry salad, and a slice of dark rye toast on it and sat next to Jordan, who'd already piled a plate and was sitting with Daniela on his lap. He'd taken Daniela's seat so that he could also sit next to Tyler.

"Uncle Jordan, can I have a cinnamon roll?" Tyler asked.

"Not if you're going to tell your mom on me. You got me in trouble." His voice took on a playful grumbling tone.

"I promise not to tell her," he said sincerely, eyes wide with his fervent promise.

"You already did, man."

"Here, Tyler," Logan said conspiratorially, sliding a piece of cinnamon roll on his son's plate. He'd taken the seat on the other side of Tyler that Grace had vacated.

"Thanks, Daddy," Tyler beamed and dug into his forbidden treat. Logan ruffled his curly dark hair.

I shook my head at the antics of these two men. These guys were putty in the hands of these two. Daniela hadn't said a word only because Jordan had already slipped her some sort of doughnut with glittery sprinkles all over it. She looked at me now with bright sprinkles all over her mouth and gave me a big smile.

"You're pretty," she said in her little voice.

"Thank you. I think you're rather pretty yourself," I smiled back at her. She was a crafty little thing. I expected her to ask me for a treat, but she asked for something else entirely.

"Can I sit on your lap?"

"Sure," I said, in surprise. Clearly done with her plate she abandoned Jordan and scrambled over into my lap.

"You have to let Lela eat, pumpkin," Jordan chided.

"Yes, Daniela. It's ok to sit in Uncle Jordan's lap while he eats, but it's not polite to do that to Lela," Logan added frowning at his daughter.

"It's fine. I'm done now," I said leaning back so she could make herself more comfortable. She sat facing me, giving me a look of awe. She ran her hand lightly along my arm.

"Look, Daddy, her arm is pretty. I want my arm to look like that," she demanded.

"She does have a pretty arm and so do you, sweetie," Logan answered.

"Her arms are the color of sunlight shining through honey," Jordan said giving me a heated gaze.

"I want honey sunshine arms," Daniela said still rubbing my arms.

"But, you have lovely sun kissed arms," I said rubbing gently on her arm.

"I do?" she asked transferring her rubbing hand to her own arm and looking at it thoughtfully.

"You sure do," I reassured her.

"Come on squirt. I have work to do, so you'll have to come to the office with me," Logan said to his daughter and then turned to his son. "Are you done eating, Tyler?"

Tyler bobbed his head up and down and scrambled off the chair.

"I want to stay with Lela," Daniela protested.

"If Daniela gets to stay with Lela, then I want to stay too," Tyler said coming over to my side.

"Lela, has to get some rest," Logan explained patiently, reaching for his daughter. "Come on. Your nanny is running late, but she'll be here any minute. Then you guys can go do something fun."

Daniela wrapped her pudgy arms tightly around my neck and pressed her head into my shoulder, giving her dad a scowl.

"I don't mind," I said in a surprised chuckle. "Really. I can stay with them until their nanny arrives."

"Are you sure?" Logan asked.

"Positive."

"Ok, well, there is a room that adjoins my office. I let them play in there when I have to work with them. You are welcome to hang out in there with them until their nanny comes. Jordan and I are just a shout away."

"Sucker," Jordan teased under his breath as he grabbed my plate, his plate, and those of his niece and nephew. I stood, still holding Daniela in my arms, while Jordan put the dishes in a dirty dish bin. Then I followed him and Logan out of the room.

I was surprised at how fascinated Daniela was with me. The two times I'd seen her prior, she would just stare at me. Tyler had given me shy glances and didn't say much, just as he was doing now. But, Daniela had never done more than just look at me from a distance. As we walked down

80

the hall Daniela ran her fingers along my face and I felt a warm, soothing, tingling sensation.

"It feels so pretty," she said in her sweet high voice.

"What feels pretty?" I heard myself saying, my voice sounded far away. I felt sluggish and slow, almost as if I was falling asleep on my feet. I looked up to see that Logan and Jordan where much further down the hall. Why were they walking so fast?

"Can I touch it?" Daniela asked. I looked down to see she was staring at me with a mesmerized expression.

"Sure," I said absently trying to clear my head. I looked down and saw Tyler walking next to me with a concerned look on his face just as Daniela began stroking the side of my face with her tiny fingers again. I could hear the murmur of Logan and Jordan's voices, but I could no longer make out what they were saying. Swiftly I felt a warm, undeniably relaxing feeling that coaxed my eyes to close and my knees to buckle. I stumbled and fell to my knees, somehow not dropping Daniela. I forced my eyes open and looked at the sweetest face looking into mine with pure innocent pleasure before I fell back and hit the floor.

Chapter 14

I thought I heard a scream. Yes, I think I did hear the scream of a little girl and rapid footsteps coming towards me. Then everyone was shouting and yelling and kids were crying? Why were they making so much noise? If I could only get my eyes open to see what was happening. I was lifted from the floor and jostled around before finally, thankfully, being put down again. There was more shouting and running.

"Lela! Lela can you hear me?" Jordan kept yelling at me. I tried to tell him yes. Didn't I say yes? I could hear him. It seemed it was he who couldn't hear me. Then it was finally quiet. Everyone just shut up at once. But, then Ethan started calling my name. He wasn't shouting like Jordan and Logan had before. At least the kids were no longer crying.

"Lela, honey, can you say something or open your eyes?" Ethan was asking me. I was going to answer, but he kept asking me before I could say anything.

"Grace! Thank goodness you're here. You have to do something." Ethan's voice sounded frantic now too. Why was everyone so frantic? A peppermint warmth began to flood my body. I was no longer floating away, though I was still tired. I was becoming less tired by the moment, and the relaxing, floaty feeling was going away. After a few more moments, my eyes fluttered open to see Grace staring down at me with a determined yet grim expression.

"Grace?" I asked in confusion.

"Yes, Lela. I'm here." Her soft, gentle voice was in direct contrast with her tense look and pursed lips.

"What is going on?" My mind was clearing now. I felt much more alert now and began to look around the room. How the hell had I ended up in Jordan's room? In Jordan's bed?

Grace sighed and stepped back. The warm, ice hot feeling stopped, and I realized she had just removed her hand from my chest.

"What the hell happened, Grace?" Jordan demanded, his face was a mingled expression of disbelief and rage.

"Apparently, Daniela was draining her life force," she answered hoarsely, looking horrified and sick.

Jordan swore. I turned my head towards the sound to see Ethan standing next to Logan and Jordan. He was looking pale and bewildered.

82

"Lela," Grace said, recapturing my attention. "Do you have pain in your head?"

"N-no," I stammered feeling confused. What were they saying? Daniela couldn't have done this. I knew what that felt like from the two times Kevin tried to kill me. It hadn't felt anything like that.

"Did you feel any pain before you passed out?"

Passed out? I didn't pass out. Did I? I could hear people talking to me. I just almost fell asleep while I was walking right?

"Lela?" Grace said looking concerned and recapturing my attention yet again.

"No, I didn't feel any pain," I mumbled belatedly.

"Ok, you need to rest now," Grace said in a soothing voice.

"Is she going to be ok?" Ethan's voice sounded strained.

"She's going to be fine. She just needs to rest." Grace sounded relieved, yet her voice was still tight. There was some sort of anguish there I realized. Then, I realized my senses were not entirely closed and shut them down. "I know I'd have to have Jordan physically removed to get him out, so he can keep watch while the rest of you get back to work."

"I'm not leaving," Jordan said through clinched teeth.

"I know that. So, you can stay with her and let me know when she wakes up. She needs to sleep. But, I want to know as soon as she wakes up if it's before I come back to check on her."

I was tired, but I wasn't asleep. Why was she talking about me sleeping?

When I opened my eyes again, the room was empty, quiet, and still. When had everyone left? I turned my head to see Jordan sitting in a chair watching me with a grim expression. Ok, so not everyone was gone.

83

"Why are you scowling at me?" I asked frowning back at him. What was he mad at me about now?

He closed his eyes, leaned forward and hung his head. He began shaking it slowly back and forth in agitation.

"Jordan?"

He looked up, his face mottled with fury, and anger, and pain.

"What's wrong?" I gasped in alarm, pushing myself into a sitting position.

He made a choked sound and laughed without humor, throwing his arms in the air. "You were right?"

"Right about what?"

"Right to want to stay away from me. You took the unknown and known risks seriously, obviously more seriously than I did."

"What are you talking about? Calm down, Jordan," I said in a low, even voice. He was beginning to freak me out. I much preferred brooding mad Jordan to this anguished, angry Jordan.

"I will not calm down!" he roared, standing so abruptly the chair he was sitting in fell backwards. I reflexively jerked back into the headboard of the bed. "You could have been killed, again! How many times have you almost been killed around me?"

The door flew open, and what appeared to be the whole Alexander clan seemed to pour in. Jordan stood there with his face distorted in anguish and his hands fisted at his sides.

"I'm fine," I said to the filling room, looking each of them in the eyes as I spoke. "We are fine. Jordan is just upset. Can you give us a moment alone?"

No one moved. They just cast wary glances between Jordan and me. I looked at Jordan and he looked back at me with the same angered

84

expression. He looked as though he wanted to beat the hell out of something or someone. But, I knew he wouldn't hurt me.

"Jordan is fine," I repeated firmly. "He's just upset. I'd really appreciate it if you'd all give us a moment."

Daisy was the first to move. She touched Ethan's arm and gave him a gentle push towards the door. Ethan looked as if he wanted to protest, but Daisy gave him a look that brooked no argument. Grace touched Logan's arm and he gave her a questioning look. Grace nodded and gestured towards the door.

"We won't be far, Lela," Logan said not looking at all convinced leaving Jordan alone with me was a good idea.

"I appreciate that, Logan," I replied never taking my eyes from Jordan's burning ones. Grace closed the door behind them and I reached a hand out to Jordan. "Come here."

He looked at my hand for a moment, then slowly walked over to the side of the bed.

"Sit down," I commanded, gesturing to the chair that someone had righted. I leaned forward, took his fisted hands into mine and then pointedly looked at the chair and then back at Jordan. He looked at me for a moment and then sat.

"Listen to me Jordan Alexander. You don't get to fall apart now that I am finally ready to stop fighting what's between us."

"She could have killed you, Lela, without even meaning to," he breathed closing his eyes. "She's a sweet, innocent child that didn't even know what she was capable of, hell none of us did."

"I don't think she was trying to harm me on purpose, Jordan. She didn't actually hurt me at all," I heard myself saying. I knew my words were true but couldn't help asking myself was I crazy? Wasn't this type of thing why I had been resisting Jordan? Wasn't this just one of the many facets of his world, that I didn't belong to, that would probably end up killing me? Yet, even knowing this, I couldn't walk away from Jordan. I was afraid. I was even terrified at my own inability to just say no to this attraction, this want, this need for him. When I tried to fight it I questioned my decision. When I decided to go with it, I questioned my decision. Either way, I never knew which decision was right. I confused myself.

"She almost killed you, Lela. And, if Ethan hadn't been here to simply keep your life force going, she probably would have." His voice was low and full of strain. "And, she's so freaked out she's inconsolable. No matter what Grace has told her, she's convinced she's done something terrible to you."

"Well, bring her in here so she can see that she didn't hurt me."

"She *did* hurt you, and I don't want her anywhere near you."

"Jordan, she's a child," I said taken aback. "Don't let her torture herself with something she doesn't understand. You have to give her little mind relief that I am ok. You can't hold it against her. If she thinks you are angry with her, she'll be devastated."

"I know she's a child, Lela. That's the point. I'm not holding it against her. I'm just being realistic. If an innocent child poses such a danger to you because I put you in this position, I am going to end up getting you killed."

"Ok, one thing at a time. Can we please put little Daniela's mind at ease so she can stop suffering. Then, I'll work on you."

"Are you telling me, you want me to let her near you again so she can finish you off?"

"No, Jordan." I shuddered at the thought of the little girl coming near me. Though I knew she'd meant no harm, I didn't want her to get

86

near me again anytime soon. "You don't have to let her near me. Just bring her in, show her that I'm ok and that you aren't upset with her."

"I've told her I'm not upset with her. I know she didn't mean it. I'm not an ogre."

"Yes, well, letting her see that I am ok and you are ok will probably help more than anything else you can do."

He just looked bleakly at me with his mingled emotions written on his face. I scooted closer to him and lifted onto my knees until I could put my arms around his neck. He pulled me gently onto his lap and buried his face in my hair. He was holding me so tight I could barely breathe, but I didn't want to say anything and send him back into his torturous mood. After a few moments, he loosened his grip slightly and let out a pent up breath.

"I'm terrified that you will come to harm because of me, but I'm too weak to let you go," Jordan murmured in my hair.

"I don't want you to let me go," I whispered back. He lifted his head and ran his fingers down the hair at the back of my head. Then he gently fisted it in his big hand and bent down to capture my mouth in a heartbreakingly sweet kiss. I melted into him, letting him release all of his pent-up anguish in this gentle, urgent kiss.

"Uh, I vote that we let Daniela see that Lela is ok so she'll stop crying. Tyler is pretty upset too," came Ethan's voice through the closed door.

"Nosy, meddling bastard," Jordan grumbled against my lips then began nibbling on them again.

"I have to agree with Ethan this time," I murmured back against his lips.

"Fine," Jordan said pulling away and trying to glare at me. But, his glare had lost a great deal of its potency. He wasn't exactly calm, but he was no longer out of control either. He stood and sat me back down on the bed. "I'll be right back."

Moments later I could hear the sounds of a sobbing child coming towards me from beyond the door.

"See. There she is. She's ok now," Jordan said, coming in the door with a very loud, tear streaked Daniela in his arms. She brushed hair and tears out of her eyes to look in the direction he was indicating. Her eyes were huge and her little faced was all flushed from crying.

"I s-s-sorry, Lela," she stammered a fresh gush of tears beginning. "I – I – I didn't mean to be bad. I didn't know – "

"I know you didn't mean it, Daniela," I was trying for a calming voice, but I had to speak loud to be heard over her balling. "You can stop crying now. I'm ok."

"You ok?" She sounded like she wasn't sure she believed me.

"Yes, I am."

"You mad at me?"

"No, Daniela. I'm not mad at you," I said, my heart breaking for the poor little thing.

"Tell Lela you won't ever touch her like that again," Jordan said sternly.

"I won't. I promise I won't. Never, ever," she said shaking her head earnestly with wide eyes pleading for Jordan to believe her as more tears gushed down her face.

"Ok, now it's time for Daisy to take you back down," he said and handed the child out the door to Daisy. Tyler's little head poked around the corner. He was holding Daisy's other hand.

"Hi, Tyler," I said smiling at him. At least I hope it was a smile. He looked at me with a deep frown on his little face as if trying to see for himself that all was well. After a moment of looking at me intently, he seemed to relax a little though his face remained serious.

"I'm sorry Daniela hurt you," he mumbled so low I could barely hear him. "She's just a brat but she didn't mean it."

This produced a new wave of waling and tears from Daniela.

"I'll be back. I'm so glad you're ok," Daisy said, poking her head around the doorframe. Then she was gone holding a balling Daniela and pulling a stern faced Tyler in her wake.

Once Daisy left with the kids, the rest of the Alexander clan came tumbling in like puppies. I hadn't realized how close I'd been, yet again, to death. Ethan was still shaken. He was a healer, but he had very limited healing ability. He could heal himself just fine but, when it came to someone else, he was no match against anything more than minor scrapes. He'd been able to do nothing more than keep my life force stable. Apparently, female healers were usually much more powerful than their male counterparts. Not that the males couldn't cultivate their abilities. They could. But, it usually came more naturally to females. It was Grace's quick return that had saved me, and this had Ethan more shaken than I had ever seen him.

Grace and Logan were especially apologetic and disturbed that it had been their child who'd almost killed me.

"We weren't sure what they could and couldn't do being the offspring of both a healer and a drainer. They haven't exhibited signs of either," Grace was explaining with pained guilt. "They've never been around regular people before. We are so sorry, Lela. We had no idea something like this could happen."

I assured them that all was fine. I really just wanted them all to stop fussing over me. My own mind was reeling. I couldn't even contemplate how I felt because I was too busy consoling all of them.

"Can I ask one thing?" Grace asked before she allowed Jordan to kick everyone out of his room. "Each time Kevin tried to drain you, you were able to resist. Why weren't you able to resist Daniela?"

"I don't know," I said thoughtfully. "Maybe, because I wasn't trying to? I had no idea I needed too. I don't know how I did it with Kevin. I felt threatened with Kevin, so I was resisting him as I would anyone else. With Daniela, I was just walking down the hallway carrying her one moment and the next I was stumbling and falling."

"You didn't feel anything?" Logan inquired.

"Actually, I did. I felt really tired all of a sudden but just cozy and warm, like I was just falling asleep on the spot. I just thought that I was tired from lack of sleep. I didn't realize that something was really wrong until I fell."

"So, you didn't feel any pain like you reported with Kevin?" Grace asked.

"No, none at all. It was actually quite a relaxing feeling."

"Very interesting," Logan murmured in deep thought.

"We'll leave now," Grace said and then turned to Jordan. "Let her rest, Jordan."

"I want to go home, Grace," I pleaded.

"It's six o'clock now. I'll check on you again at eight. If all is well, Jordan can take you home. For now, you rest."

Six o'clock? We'd finished eating a little before eleven-thirty this morning. I'd been out for almost seven hours?

90

"Jordan can fill you in on what's happening with the case. We had to make some moves without you and we need you up to speed," Logan added and then followed his wife out of the door.

Jordan closed the door and then climbed onto the bed next to me. I was propped up on all of his pillows so he just leaned back against the headboard.

"Are you sure you aren't doing these things on purpose?" I gave him a sideways, narrow eyed glance.

"Doing what things on purpose?" He frowned in confusion.

"Well, I keep having people try to kill me, but I seem to always wake up in your bed," I tried to tease. I couldn't deal with anymore of Jordan's brooding. "You told me to go rest in your bed this morning and I said no. Yet, here I am."

"Don't even joke about it," he snorted without humor.

"Then, tell me what happened while I was, uh, resting."

He rested his head back against the headboard and filled me in. Logan had felt that they were missing something. Out of the three visitors Kevin had received and we'd interviewed, the college student was the one that didn't fit. So, Logan had given the professor a call. It turned out that the college professor didn't know anything about any of his students planning to interview Kevin, nor had he approved it. Each student had to turn in a preliminary case study for approval and no one had turned in one on Kevin. He assured Logan that even if they had, he wouldn't have allowed it. According to Professor Grier, none of his students were even aware of Kevin because the case was ongoing and wasn't currently in the discoverable records nor on his list of possible subjects to do reports on for his students.

"So we pulled him back in for a second questioning. Two other agents had to handle that interview since we were all here, but the kid, James Sucre, told them that he was hired by another student to do the report on Kevin," Jordan explained. "He specifically told James who to do the report on and what questions to ask. James said he needed the extra money so he sometimes does reports for lazy students who pay him to do theirs."

"Who is this other student that is too lazy to do his own report?" I asked.

"We don't know yet. The name he gave the kid is not one on Professor Grier's roster, nor anywhere else we've searched. Our student, James, says he delivered the report to the mystery student Monday and he hasn't seen him since. He also said that the student told him to ask Kevin if he knew about the Jason Walker case. He told him that question was really important and he wouldn't pay him unless he brought back the answer."

"That's our dead suspect from the video," I said in surprise.

"Exactly."

"So, what is the plan now?" I asked with a growing excitement at the prospect of uncovering yet another layer of this case. It was official. I either had a death wish, I was crazy, or maybe both. I'd almost been killed again, yet I was sitting in on interrogations of the man who'd tried to kill me twice. Though I was afraid, I could feel this maniacal need to continue the case. Nothing ever happened to me until I got around the Alexanders. Maybe I was a thrill seeker and I didn't know it.

"Where did you go?" Jordan asked frowning.

"I'm sorry. What were you saying?" I asked, refocusing my attention on Jordan.

"I hadn't really said anything yet. What were you thinking?"

"I was just thinking about the case. What are we going to do now?"

He didn't look like he totally believed me but he continued.

"Logan has all possible resources looking for this mystery student. The kid gave us a sketch. He's pretty certain that the kid is telling the truth. If he was as confused as you say he was at the first interview, then we are pretty confident he was just used to get information to and from Kevin. After seeing the sketch, the professor says that the mystery student doesn't look familiar either. We are going to have to go back to Kevin, but Logan is hoping we will find this student first. We don't have a lot of time, so if we don't locate him in the next few hours we are going to have to go at Kevin without the added pressure of having his accomplice in custody."

"What time is Logan thinking of interrogating Kevin again. I'm ready, I can do it."

"You *are* crazy," he said looking exasperated. "You nearly die and all you can think about is going to Kevin's interrogation? Are you becoming an adrenaline junkie?"

"No, I'm not," I said calmly and tried to sound reasonable. "But, we don't have a lot of time, as you just pointed out. If I can help, then I want to help."

"Well, Grace said you are basically fine but just weak," he said grudgingly. "She is leaving it up to you after eight pm. You've been sleeping mostly since around 11 this morning. Grace says you also recovered much faster this time then you did from Kevin's two attacks. She's not sure why. But, she says you'll likely be very tired for the next 24 hours and sleep a lot."

I was really tired. Usually when I felt like this, I either hadn't slept well for the last few days or I was catching a cold. When I don't sleep well for several days it's usually due to lack of cardio. Hitting the elliptical or some other high energy cardio is the fastest cure. When I have been hitting the cardio regularly and I feel this tired, I'm usually trying to catch a cold. Considering I wasn't having any sleeping problems, I figured rest was the best medicine. If I didn't rest I wouldn't be ready to help with the case when they needed me. Though I would have felt more comfortable in my own bed, I pushed my feelings of awkwardness regarding commandeering Jordan's bedroom away and lay back down. It was only two more hours before eight. Jordan had work to do so he didn't stay more than about another half hour. And within moments of him closing the door I was sound asleep.

Chapter 15

If Grace came back to check on me at eight, I didn't wake up. The next time I opened my eyes it was in response to Daisy calling my name. I opened my eyes to see her sitting in the chair Jordan had left by the bed and leaning towards me.

"How are you feeling?" she whispered.

"I'm fine. What time is it?"

"Its eleven o'clock," she whispered, switching on a bedside lamp.

"What's happening? Are we going to interview Kevin?" I asked squinting from the glow of light.

"If you are up for it. We can't wait any longer," she said looking me over critically and putting her hand lightly on my arm. "Grace told me to check and see if you were up for it. The interrogation shouldn't take long. Still, we don't want you pushing yourself."

I pushed myself up to a seated position. "I'm good. I am a little tired but not overly so. I've gone to work feeling more tired than this."

"I think you're right," she said removing her hand from my arm. "Well, like I said, it shouldn't take too long. We just want to know how Kevin reacts when he finds out we know how he ordered the hit on Walker. If you can get any words or fleeting thoughts it would be great. Or, if you can figure out why he ordered the hit that would be even better."

"Give me just a few minutes," I said running my hands through my hair. I was still dressed from this morning. I'd been placed on Jordan's bed with a blanket thrown over me instead of stripped and redressed this time, thank goodness. The only thing that had been removed was my shoes. However, Daisy reminded me that I had to wear some of her or Grace's clothes and I quickly changed into the clothes she provided.

"I know you said that Kevin was surprised and confused when we first told him about the kidnapping but, for him to order a hit, he must know something," Daisy stated once we were in the car and on our way. "We think that he learned something through his mystery student and that's why he ordered the hit. We've analyzed the specific questions that James Sucre asked and the paper he wrote. We think there's something there. We're hoping that you will be able to pick up more this time that will shed light on exactly what's happening."

"I'll do my best."

Once again, I walked into the observation room and assumed my position in the stool against the wall right next to the glass. As before, Jordan handed me pen and paper and he and Daisy remained beside me. This was becoming routine. Ethan and Logan escorted Kevin in, sat him down and jumped right in.

"We know about James Sucre, Kevin," Logan was saying. "We know he was hired, unwittingly to give you a message and take your message back. We also know you ordered the hit on Walker."

Kevin's reaction was so surprising I almost didn't write it down. He was feeling anger and betrayal. But what surprised me most were his feelings of protectiveness. Who was he trying to protect? I scribbled the words anger, betrayal and protectiveness as Logan went on.

"It's only a matter of time before we find your guy Kevin," Logan continued. "And, then you will be implicated in Beck's kidnapping. I hope no harm comes to him because you already have enough trouble to deal with."

Kevin was seething. *Can't find him, not before he finds the others*, ran across his mind and I jerked. He was very agitated. Before his mind was more blank and controlled. He was even thinking in clear words. And, he was clearly concerned about protecting someone. The two remaining suspects in the sketches he'd provided? But, if they were responsible for the kidnapping he'd ordered, then why was he after them? They were part of his organization after all.

"Ask him why he had Mr. Beck kidnapped and then is killing off the kidnappers," I thought to Logan. Moments later, Logan repeated the question.

"I didn't have anyone kidnapped. How many times do I have to tell you that?" Kevin bit out. And then I heard the rest of the thought he hadn't spoken. *I'm trying to save them. And you idiots are going to get her killed.*

The image of Mrs. Beck came to his mind and realization slammed into me. He was trying to protect Mrs. Beck! He was telling the truth when he said he didn't have anyone kidnapped. I could feel his frustration with it.

Logan was talking so I switched to Ethan. *"Tell him, if he didn't have Mr. Beck kidnapped then someone sure is trying to make him look guilty for it."*

Ethan smoothly cut Logan off repeating my words. Daisy and Jordan glanced curiously at me and then looked back at the glass.

No shit, came Kevin's mental thought. *And if you cocksuckers catch my man, they'll succeed. I need to get the hell out of here. I've got to get to her.*

I was so confused I didn't know where to go from here. Ok, he was trying to protect her. I didn't have another question to ask. After a moment I decided I could only just let Logan and Ethan know what I knew. Maybe they would know what to ask next.

"He wants to protect Mrs. Beck. He believes he's being set up to take the fall for something. He wants to get to her to protect her," I thought to Logan and then Ethan. Silence reined while they both digested this new information. Again, Daisy and Jordan turned and looked at me.

"If you help us then we can help you," Ethan finally said. Complete and utter distrust filtered through Kevin's mind.

"He doesn't trust or believe you," I thought first to Ethan and then Logan. *"Maybe assure him that Mrs. Beck is being relocated to somewhere else where you can keep her safe from his men."*

Logan said my words out loud, but they had a violently opposite reaction than what I was expecting. I don't know what he looked like outwardly, but inwardly that put Kevin in a panic.

No dammit. They can't know we are on to them or they will kill them all for sure. And, I'll be completely fucked! Fucking Alexanders! We have to take them out before they know we are on to them.

Then his mind began to scramble as if trying to figure out what to do.

"Uh, that sent him into a tailspin," I thought to Logan and relayed the thoughts I'd picked up from Kevin.

"I can see that makes you nervous," Logan said, his voice now low, menacing and mean. I'd never heard Logan sound so brutal. It was rather disconcerting. "But, understand this, Kevin. I don't know what you have to do with this, but we will not let Mrs. Beck and her children come to harm. And you better pray to whatever hell you come from that nothing happens to Mr. Beck. I know that you could help end this. So, I will move heaven and earth to make sure you pay in every way possible if that woman loses her husband and those girls lose their father because of you."

"You can't move her," Kevin growled.

"Why the hell not," Logan growled right back.

"I don't trust you for a minute, Logan Alexander," Kevin spat. "The only way I can be sure I won't go down for this too is to make sure my witnesses are left alive to speak for me. If I tell you anything, you'll save the Becks and still make sure I go down for it."

"If anything happens to Mr. Beck, you better hope I keep you alive to stand trial for the crimes you're already in here for." Logan's voice held such brutality and coldness a chill went down my spine.

"You weren't concerned about who sent me to kill that Lela girl, but you expect me to believe you won't set me up here no matter what I do," Kevin spat out. I jerked and Jordan stiffened at his words.

"Oh, I'm very interested. Only, I'm not sure that anybody sent you. I have a hard time believing that any man who would brutalize a woman and attempt to rape her while he drained her life force was simply acting on orders." Logan's voice was barely a whisper. "Especially since

98

we know that you are in a position to give orders, not receive them. I think Walkers death confirms that."

Fury and the flicker of a thought crossed Kevin's mind. He couldn't dispute Logan's words. But, his mind flickered back to an image and broken words of someone ordering him to take me out. *Seduce her so there is no trace of foul play.* Only, he hadn't been able to get near me.

From what I could gather from his racing and disjointed thoughts, if he'd openly come on to me and we'd been dating, the Alexanders would know my life force had been drained even if regular doctors could not figure it out. If I'd been drained brutally, I might have had a heart attack, stroke or some other obvious cause of death that would have been the result of a brutal draining. But, if I had submitted to him, I would have just inexplicably died. Modern medicine would find it a puzzle with no answers. But, the Alexanders would have known and he would have been their first suspect. When he'd brought this to his superior, he was told to get it done one way or another. The rage he felt now stemmed from the realization that this had been the beginning of his set up by someone in his own organization. Someone was trying to get rid of him.

I quickly also realized that this was the difference between Kevin's two attacks on me and little Daniela's inadvertent attempt to drain my life force. I had felt terrible pain with Kevin because I was trying to resist him yes, but also because I believe he would have tried to be more brutal in the end to force some sort of strain that would be discoverable by doctors as the cause of death. Daniela had just been curious and attracted to whatever my life force appeared to be for her. Kevin had been trying to control me with pain and also provide a cause of death that wouldn't point so easily to him.

Refocusing my attention back on the current interview, I relayed all of these new revelations regarding Kevin and the case to Logan and Ethan. I could contemplate my newest revelations about the attempts to drain me later.

"You either talk, or I give the order to move her now," Logan threatened.

There was a tense silence in the room beyond while Kevin thought about this.

"What's it going to be," Ethan snapped.

"Don't move her," Kevin said, giving in angrily. He'd decided to go out on a limb, unable to figure out how to accomplish saving the Becks by himself. Just maybe the Alexanders wouldn't double cross him. He didn't have many options. And, no matter what happened to him, he wouldn't let anything happen to Mrs. Beck. "I don't know where Mr. Beck is, but I'll tell you what I know."

As Kevin spoke, I was wide eyed with what his feelings were telling me. He was in love with Mrs. Beck. I shuttered at the contrast between this brutal man and his feelings for her. What was even scarier was that I was pretty sure she had no idea.

"We're listening," Logan said.

"Mrs. Beck is my accountant. She handles all of my money. Long story that's not important right now. The same person that had her husband kidnapped is the same person that ordered me to kill the Lela girl. You likely picked up his scent at the site you found not far from where your boy here got shot."

I assumed he was gesturing to Ethan since he was the one who'd been shot.

"Why would he order Lela killed and then kidnap Mr. Beck," Ethan asked skeptically.

"The two incidents aren't exactly related," Kevin explained. "He thought the girl was one of your spies like this guy here. He wasn't sure if she'd seen him and could identify him. We weren't sure how long she'd been hanging around. So, he just needed to make sure she couldn't identify him and that no one had made a sketch of him. Even with a sketch, you would have needed her to make an ID if you ever caught up with him. I had not been there so you wouldn't have gotten my scent. So I wouldn't have triggered the alarm being around the ranch. I was also already planted at your ranch for other reasons."

"What does any of this have to do with Mr. Beck?" Logan asked.

"After they realized that I was the only suspect in regards to that girl, and you guys thought I was running things, they needed to make me disappear. Mrs. Beck is my personal accountant. The amount of money they want is exactly how much I have that she has access to. I'm being framed for the kidnapping, and if they succeed, I will take the fall for it while they wipe me out financially. The only way she can come up with that type of money is if she uses my money. And, the only reason they haven't made her hand it over is because you must have your people around her."

"How does that protect your so called boss? What if we believe you and start looking for him?" Ethan snorted. "Taking you out would seem like the best plan of action."

"They already know that you think I ordered the kidnapping. As long as they believe that you guys aren't looking for them, Mrs. Beck is fairly safe for now. They are waiting for an opening in your defenses of her to get in and give her the instructions to take my money, no doubt. They know you don't suspect anyone else because you would have moved her if you didn't think you had your guy. And, I have no doubt they are trying to kill me. That is why I have refused all visitors except the ones I had. I needed to know what was going on when you told me about the kidnapping. They didn't know either, as far as I could tell, but I got enough information about the operations in motion and what was happening to figure it out for myself."

"This doesn't make sense? Why would they bother taking your money?" Ethan asked, still not sounding remotely convinced.

"This is what we do," Kevin sneered. "Robbing, kidnapping for ransom, stealing priceless items. Why wouldn't they try to take my money and get rid of me? I'm sure they figure I won't have a need for it once they figure out how to kill me. I'm an easy score."

"If Mrs. Beck is your personal accountant then why doesn't she know who you are?" Logan asked.

"She knows me as Kenneth Wise," Kevin said. "And no, that's not my real name either."

"What makes you think they will kill her if we move her?" Ethan asked.

"Because they told her not to involve anyone. If they frame me for ordering the kidnapping and have to kill her because she's involved you, they'll do it. They know you're involved, but you're pinning it on me. The moment they think you are looking for another suspect, she's dead. And, most of my actual crew will be craftily implicated. They may not get my money, but I'll still be in here until they can figure out a way to kill me. Trust me, they know she's being watched by you guys. They just know I'm the scapegoat right now. If you move her they will know that you guys no longer think I'm your man."

"Yea but if you are in here, how can they frame you for the kidnapping?" Ethan prompted.

"The same way you would build a case against me. You already traced Walker back to me. But, I'm not Walker's handler. He wouldn't do anything on my orders. The two other guys I gave you the sketches for were working with Walker. The college kid was sent by the only person I know I could trust."

"And you let him know that Walker was behind the kidnapping, but then you had him taken out?" Ethan sounded puzzled.

"I didn't have Walker taken out. His handler did so that he could pin this whole thing on me when you guys figured out he was from the same organization. I'm sure the evidence was easy to find in order to connect us."

"We're done for now," Logan interjected, cutting the interrogation off. "We'll check into what you're saying. You'd better be telling the truth for your sake."

Once Kevin was taken away, Logan and Ethan joined us in the interrogation room.

"That was awesome," Ethan grinned at me and then turned to Daisy and Jordan. "She was totally talking in our heads."

"It was rather timely and useful information," Logan said looking pleased. "I think we got all that we needed to get for now. We're looking in the wrong place if this is accurate and I need to change a few things around with our guys out working leads. How is your energy?"

"I'm fine," I beamed back at them. It had been a rather awesome experience.

"She's dead on her feet," Daisy said scrutinizing me. "If you think you have everything then, I suggest that Jordan take her home so she can sleep."

"I'm fine, Daisy. Really."

"Actually that's just adrenaline talking," Daisy retorted.

"No, that's fine. No need for a debriefing," Logan interjected. "If we have any questions, we'll call. Take her home, Jordan."

Chapter 16

Moments later I was bustled into Jordan's SUV and on my way home. Before even pulling away from the building I must have fallen asleep, because the next thing I knew Jordan was opening my door and lifting me out of the car.

"Oh, I must have fallen asleep," I mumbled as he straightened with me in his arms. "I can walk."

"I don't want you to walk. That would mean I'd have to put you down," he murmured into my hair. What was it about my hair? He seemed to always be nuzzling in it. I thought to ask him, but I was too comfortable in his arms. I handed him my keys, burrowed against his solid chest, and started to doze again.

I woke completely however when he brought me into my bedroom and placed me on the bed. I needed to take a shower. For some reason I never slept well without a shower or a bath before bed. I dragged myself into the bathroom with my pajamas and rushed through my shower and teeth brushing. Jordan had apparently done the same in the hall bathroom because his hair was wet and he was dressed in pajamas and laying on my bed when I came out of the bathroom.

"Uh, what are you doing?"

"I'm going to sleep," he said not opening his eyes.

"But, you're in *my* bed."

"You sleep in mine all the time, so I didn't think you'd mind," he said grinning, but he still didn't open his eyes. It was so weird seeing him in my bed. It did weird things to me that I was much too tired to contemplate at the moment.

He opened one eye and squinted at me. "I just want to sleep, Lela. Well, that's not totally true, but I'm too tired to do anything but sleep. I'd rather sleep in here with you. But, if you aren't comfortable with it I can sleep in the living room."

What the hell. I was too tired to care. Though I wasn't totally comfortable with this arrangement, I had decided to give this me and Jordan thing a try, right? Sleeping wasn't much to ask for. I slid into the bed next to him and he threw an arm around me. In less than a minute he was out.

I must have fallen off to sleep right after Jordan. The next conscious thing I was aware of was a delicious ache in my breasts and between my legs. As I became aware of my body and its surroundings, I realized it was already more alert then my mind was. Sunlight was filtering through my bedroom window and I was spooned in Jordan's arms with my back to his front. He had me flush up against him and leaning back into him. The arm wrapped under me was wreaking havoc with my breasts while his other hand had found its way into my pajama pants and was stroking me masterfully. I was hot and wet and my breathing was picking up. The thought flittered through my mind that I should probably stop this, but my body was way ahead of my mind. My legs were even open for him allowing him free access that I hadn't knowingly permitted. I finally opened my mouth to protest just as he slid a

105

finger inside me and then slowly out and around that most sensitive part of me. Nothing but a groan of pleasure escaped. This had to stop. I wasn't ready for this.

"I see you are awake now, I can hear your mind going," he cooed into my neck.

"Jordan I – " I began sounding breathy to my own ears. My heart was pounding, I was so turned on. How could he get me so turned on so fast?

"Shh," he breathed into my ear. "Relax, Lela."

"But – "

"Stop being a control freak," he said evenly as he trailed kisses along my jaw and throat. His skilled fingers never stopped their relentless and sweet torture. "Relax."

I was panting now and completely out of control. I realized distractedly that I was gripping both of his arms with my hands and holding on for dear life. My hips were moving in tandem to the rhythm of his fingers between my legs of their own accord. Somewhere in the far reaches of my mind, there was a voice screaming for me to hold onto my control and stop this, but it was being drowned out by the vortex of sensation that was claiming me.

"Jordan, I – I can't."

"Yes you can. Come for me, baby," he whispered urgently in my ear as he began stroking me in a way that made my body jerk and writhe against his hand. "Let go of your control for just a moment."

Jordan bit me lightly on the shoulder as he continued his relentless stroking, and I cried out as waves of a delicious ecstasy overrode my control and flooded me with irresistible sensation after sensation that I was helpless to stop. My body trembled, fully engulfed in carnal pleasure, and

I lost all thought. It seemed to go on forever as Jordan crooned in my ear and held me while still stroking me.

"Thank you," he said softly in my ear when I finally began to calm down.

"For what?" I asked, still breathing a little harshly and my heart was still pounding.

"For giving up some of your control, even if just for a moment."

I turned my head in confusion and looked at him over my shoulder, and he captured my mouth and kissed me deeply. Once he finally released my lips, he gently extricated his hands from my pants and breasts and rolled off the bed. Feeling vulnerable now, though I was still fully clothed, I pulled the covers up over me and looked at him. He stared back looking very tense.

"Are you leaving?" I asked, swallowing my insecure feelings and trying to sound only curious.

"No, I just have to put some distance between us or we may end up doing more than you are ready for."

"I don't understand," I asked puzzled. I knew he wanted me. I'd felt his erection pressing into my back. Wasn't the whole point of him ambushing me and turning me on in my sleep to get under my defenses and have his way with me?

"Can you honestly say that you are ready for me to make love to you right now?"

Hell yes I was ready, but I didn't say that. I didn't say anything. My body was more than willing and ready, but I was already feeling vulnerable at how he'd so completely taken over my body and overrode my defenses.

"You see? I think that you have some reservations," he continued after a moment. "And, even though you might be turned on enough to let me now, you'd have some regrets or concerns after that would make you pull away from me again. You're just now allowing me to even talk about us having a relationship, let alone touch you. You are too much of a control freak to give yourself to me so easily without any repercussions."

"I am not a control freak," I defended weakly. Was I a control freak?

"Yes you are," he grinned with humor and understanding in his eyes. It was a bit disconcerting that he seemed to really get me. Was he seriously planning to wait? There was some truth to what he said. Even though my libido was jumping up and down, I don't think I would react well after if we made love now.

"Why do you say that?" I asked, refocusing on a safer topic. "I don't try to control people."

"No. You don't. But, you hold rigid control over yourself and your surroundings. You are rigidly self-possessed. I don't know what kind of process you have to go through, but until you make up your mind to let something or someone in, then they stay on the outside."

I was taken aback, not only at his assessment of me but, by the eerily accurate ring of truth in it. I'd never thought of myself as a controlling person, but I was very clear on what I wanted and didn't want in my life, day to day and long term. But, a control freak?

"Why do you think that?" I asked, wanting to know how he came to such a conclusion.

"Because I want you and I know you want me. But, whenever I tried to act on our mutual desire before, you would shut me down. Hell, you shut me out completely."

"So just because I wouldn't sleep with you, I'm a control freak?"

"Ok, maybe control freak is too strong a description. But, I know you are just as attracted to me and want me as much as I want you. I also know that you resist it and fight it. I've spent a lot of time trying to figure out why. I thought about how responsive you were in my arms from the first time I kissed you. This thing between us is not easy to resist, yet you do. Then, I thought about what you told me when I asked you when the last time was that you'd dated anyone. You told me it had been 2 years."

"So what. Just because I don't sleep around doesn't mean I'm a control freak," I grumbled.

"It's more than that, Lela. You don't even date. How could a woman as sensual and responsive as you not date?"

"I hadn't found anyone I wanted to date."

He came and sat on the edge of the bed. "Admit it, what you feel for me terrifies you because it makes you feel out of control."

He was right. I didn't want to admit it, but I certainly couldn't deny it. I could admit it to myself though. What I felt for him absolutely terrified me. I definitely felt like, if I gave into my feelings for him, I would be swept away and might not be able to find my way back. I would be at his mercy.

"See, even now you can't admit it but you know it's true," he said giving me a knowing grin. "I also think it has something to do with the envelope you tore up yesterday."

"What are you talking about?" I asked taken off guard by the change in subject.

"Yesterday, when you were flipping through your mail, there was a card that you didn't bother to open. You looked at the return address and then ripped it up and threw it away."

I remembered now. The card from my mother. Why did he have to be so perceptive and observant? I did not read the cards from my mother. I simply tried to stay away from her. Her cards were always heartfelt pleas to try and reconnect, though any hint of a true apology or remorse were carefully avoided. I'd fallen for them too many times. And every time she would be on her best behavior for a while and then the whining and complaining would start. I had to listen to all her whining and complaining about everyone and everything. And if I didn't agree with her or listen then she would get an attitude. Every little thing my father did made her angry and I had to hear how much she hated him or some other such nonsense. If I tried to interject some reasoning then I was accused of not understanding, having an attitude or being mean. When I tried to put distance between us and not react to her whining then her attacks would turn to me. I was mean and had no feeling. If that didn't work then she escalated and I was a mean, heartless, bitch or something of the sort, and she ran to tell all the friends she'd previously been talking bad about what a bad daughter I was. She was toxic and I found it much better for my own sanity to stay away from her.

"Lela?"

"Yea," I replied briskly. Jordan's voice jerked me from the negative thoughts of my mother.

"Who was the card from?" he asked quietly.

I sighed, "My mother."

He looked surprised for a moment. Clearly that wasn't the answer he was expecting.

"I never hear you talk about your parents."

"There isn't much to say."

"Why did your mother send you a card?"

"Because, if she called, she knows I wouldn't answer the phone," I said tensing up. The heat he'd created now gone.

"Why?"

"I don't really want to talk about her, Jordan," I said and started to scoot to the other edge of my bed so I could stand up. He grabbed my hand and gently pulled me towards him.

"Am I correct in thinking that this also has a lot to do with your iron clad, cool, self-controlled, self – possessed personality?"

"Let's just say you may be on to something and move on, shall we?"

"Ok. For now. And, I'll also try to wait for you to come to terms with the idea of making love with me."

I didn't respond. I just pulled my hand and he released it.

"Hopefully I will be able to hurry it along before I spontaneously combust," he grimaced and then changed the subject. "And, you'd better call in and make arrangements to be out of the office today. You need to rest. Logan thinks we may need you again once they finish following up on all of the latest information Kevin gave us. Time is running short. It's already Thursday."

"What are you getting ready to do?" I asked.

"I'm going to go fix us some coffee and breakfast. We also need to eat."

He stood and headed for the door. I lay back down, thinking of what he said. Was I really a control freak? I did take great pains to control my own environment. I wasn't sure how I felt about him seeing so deeply into me. Then I laughed out loud at the thought. I guess I was a control freak. I'd always thought of a control freak as someone who tried to control everyone and everything. I had no illusions that I could control anyone else. As I have often said when asked for advice, you can't control other people you can only control the degree to which they affect you and your life.

"Uh oh, what are you thinking about so intently?"

I looked up to see Jordan standing in my bedroom doorway holding a mug of coffee and frowning.

"I was just thinking about what you said. I have to admit there is some truth to it."

"Don't think about it now. Drink this," he said handing me the mug. "I have food on the stove and, if you think too hard about it right now, I won't be able to counteract your overthinking everything."

I opened my mouth to protest but he stopped me with a kiss. Once he was sure I wasn't going to argue with him, he put the mug in my hand and headed out the door.

"I'm aware of your distraction method. Don't think I'm not," I yelled at the empty doorway.

"Of course you are aware because you think too much," came his teasing reply.

Just as we were finishing up breakfast, Jordan's phone rang. It was Logan and he wanted us back at the ranch.

"Yes, she slept all the way home and then all night," he reassured Logan. "She didn't wake up until about 10 this morning and she's doing fine."

He gave me a slow, wicked grin that had my cheeks flaming and my stomach fluttering just thinking about how I'd been awakened this morning.

Chapter 17

"We went to talk to Mrs. Beck last night and she does indeed know Kevin as Kenneth Wise." Logan said, beginning our meeting. He was standing and pacing at the front of the conference room. "Once we told her that we believed something Kenneth Wise was involved in was the reason her husband was kidnapped, we were able to obtain all of his records, including those of his various properties. We've sent teams to check it out, however, we don't believe that Mr. Beck is being held at one of Kevin's properties. If Kevin is telling the truth about not having anything to do with the kidnapping, and thanks to Lela we believe he is, then Mr. Beck is likely being held at another property owned by the organization or one of its members. We need a list of the organization's properties, so we went back and talked to Kevin again last night."

"Without me?" I blurted out not thinking. Jordan smiled.

"We're all very tired and we don't need nearly as much sleep as you do, Lela." Logan's voice was understanding and apologetic. "We also weren't almost killed. Grace felt, and we all agreed, that you needed to rest. We'd gotten quite a lot already thanks to you."

I tried for gracious acceptance at being left out of the loop last night and said nothing.

"Told you she'd be mad," Ethan laughed. "I'm telling you, she's hooked."

I stuck my tongue out at him. He winked.

"Anyway," Logan continued. The corner of his mouth was twitching. "We allowed Kevin to make contact with his man, he refused to give us a name. He said that his man wouldn't come to him directly because the higher ups would know something was wrong. Basically, he is Kevin's equal within the organization, like two managers in a company. Only, they aren't encouraged to know each other. They all run separate

113

operations. That way, if one gets taken down like Kevin, it's not so easy to tie them to anyone else in the organization. Nevertheless, Kevin and this guy became friends and started watching each other's backs. He would know that Kevin got taken down but wouldn't bother to go see him under normal circumstances. That's why he sent the kid. So, we've arranged for the kid to meet with him again and pass along the information."

"Kevin says he already has his guy looking at each of the properties, but there are so many of them it's going too slow," Ethan said, taking over the telling. "And, since he has to do it covertly and can't involve anyone in his unit, he hasn't made much progress. So, he's going to have his guy give us a list of the properties so we can start checking them out too."

"How did you get him to agree to that?" Jordan asked skeptically.

"Logan was very persuasive," Ethan said smugly. "I don't think he trusts us, but I think he knows that we want Mr. Beck back safely. And, I think he understands now that if that doesn't happen things will be much worse for him than they are now."

"So what happens now?" I asked.

"We wait to hear from Ricky and Beto. They are shadowing the kid to make sure he comes out of this alive," Logan answered. "Once we get the list of properties, we will need everyone on this. It's Thursday already. We need to end this. We'll be putting you and Lela on a team looking at the more vacant properties. I suspect that if the plot against Kevin isn't well known, then whomever is setting him up doesn't want everyone to know that the kidnapped victim he's being blamed for is in one of their more obscure and lesser used properties."

"How will you know which are the more vacant properties?" Jordan asked.

"Once we get the list, we'll be talking to Kevin again. He should be familiar enough with them since they all apparently use them from time to time for whatever crimes they are in the process of committing. We also had Kevin give us the address of this mystery person he thinks is framing him. We're having some of our information teams find out what name the home is listed under and find any other properties under that name. He may very well have Mr. Beck being held in one of his personal properties. Kevin has quite a few personal properties himself, so this guy might also."

"What would I be doing at the more vacant properties?" I asked confused. It wasn't like I could storm into a building full of these drainers and rescue anyone.

"We want you to see how many minds you can make out and what they are thinking. With any luck, you might be able to identify Mr. Beck's mind or find out where he is."

"Why not just take me to this guy you suspect's address to see if I can figure it out by listening to his mind?" I asked.

"We might just end up doing that," Logan said. "So far he hasn't been at his home address, and we don't know where he is. But, if he shows up, we'll definitely be taking you there. For now, we need you on standby."

So, I was sent home to twiddle my thumbs only Daisy was with me now. Jordan was needed now since he'd gotten some sleep. I was a bit miffed at this. Everyone else got to help but me. And, I'd even taken a day off of work.

"Wow, I can hear you pouting all the way over here," Daisy said in feigned horror.

"I'm not pouting."

"Oh, well whatever you're doing over there that looks a lot like pouting, I can practically hear it from here. I think I may actually hear specific words," she teased.

"Shut up," I said trying not to smile. "I just want to be useful. I just feel like I've been benched and I want to play the game."

"I told you that you would like working for us." She looked at me sideways with a smug grin before turning her attention back to the road.

"Yea, yea."

"Have you talked to Blake lately?" Daisy asked, seemingly out of the blue.

"Uh, yea. I talk to him, or at least text him, almost every day. Why?" I asked, now giving her a sideways glance.

"I was just wondering. He hasn't been home in a couple of weeks. I figured he'd be home soon."

"He will be home soon, but why do you care? Are you crushing on my brother, Daisy?" I teased.

"I was just asking when he'd be home," she said trying to sound nonchalant. "We are in the middle of an investigation. If he comes home before it's over, we need to know what to tell him. I'm just covering all of the basis, that's all."

That wasn't all, but she did have a point. I'd had my suspicions for a while now that Daisy had a thing for my brother. I knew Blake had a thing for her. And, he would be home sometime tomorrow. I guess we would have to tell him something if they were going to be coming to get me in the middle of the night. I hadn't thought much of it since no one was actually after me like last time.

"He'll be home sometime tomorrow. He knows the Alexander Ranch is my account. I guess I could just pretend that I was going to work each day as usual when you guys need me."

"True," Daisy said absently. "Unless we need you in the middle of the night."

"Yea, that could be tricky," I agreed since I'd just been thinking the same thing.

"Well, I'll bring it to Logan's attention and we'll work on some possible stories," she shrugged.

The day ticked by. I took a nap since I was still a bit tired. Then I did laundry and cleaned up. Daisy was busy on her laptop for a while and then she crashed on the couch. When she finally woke up, I was in my room reading. I couldn't remember the last time I was able to spend a good part of a day reading. Though I felt guilty, I told myself it was a well-deserved guilty pleasure. I was not just playing hooky from work, I was on - call. Besides, I'd made arrangements to make sure nothing would be neglected if I were out of the office for a week, which I wouldn't be.

I was into the story deep when I heard Daisy start down the hallway towards me. I looked up as she entered my room and flopped down beside me on the bed. Then she wrinkled her nose.

"Do you know your bed smells like Jordan?" she frowned and then raised a brow.

"Uh, no I didn't. I don't smell anything, but Jordan did lay on my bed just as you are now," I said smoothly. I wasn't going to be embarrassed. Nothing happened. Well, almost nothing.

"So, you and Jordan sat in here like this and chatted like girlfriends?" she asked, her lips twitching with amusement at her not funny teasing.

117

"Something like that," I answered noncommittally.

"That's not what my nose is telling me." She looked as though she were going to burst out laughing at any moment.

"What do you mean what your nose is telling you?" I said with a bit of irritation. "What is it you think you smell?"

She was trying to needle me but she was wrong. I knew what she was getting at, but nothing had happened. Well, maybe not nothing but not what she was insinuating. She was back to frowning again.

"On second thought, I don't think I want to analyze this too closely. We are talking about Jordan here." She shivered as if the idea was gross. Then her eyes lit up. "Wait until I tell Ethan!"

"There's nothing to tell," I said, shoving her. She sat up and crossed her legs, laughing at me.

"Do you really believe your own lies or do you just think we do?" She asked wryly.

"You know what Daisy," I said giving her the finger. Ok, it wasn't something I'd normally do but she was starting to annoy me.

"Whoa! Ok. I'll leave you alone," she said laughing. Seeing that I didn't exactly think it was funny though she settled. "You know I'm just teasing you right?"

"Yes. I'm aware of that," I gritted out.

"I'm just happy for you guys, that's all. And, I know how skittish you are. I just want things to work out for you both. And, since you won't talk to me about it, I don't know what's going on."

Skittish? I wasn't skittish. Was I?

"You don't need to know. It's none of your business," I said with no real heat behind it. "What are you, Jordan's mother hen?"

118

"Nope. Just looking out for two stubborn people I care about who won't talk to me," She sighed. "Besides, it's not like my love life is so interesting."

"Maybe, that's because you're too busy meddling in mine," I said sweetly.

She frowned at my bed again and stood up.

"Well, I think I will get some work done on my laptop since you aren't feeling very hospitable right now," she sniffed. I chuckled as she walked out of my room with her nose in the air.

I hadn't heard from Blake yesterday, so I gave him a call. He didn't pick up. I left a message and hung up. He'd likely call tonight.

Chapter 18

By evening there was still no word. Jordan had arrived around five-thirty and watched television on the DVR with us. I'd been disappointed that he hadn't brought any news. Clearly it was a waiting game for us, but they didn't seem to be bothered by all the waiting. Maybe because they were used to it. After all, this was their job. When they weren't on duty they hung out and had fun or worked on the ranch. No one would ever know that they were in the middle of a kidnapping case.

"Alright. What's eating you?" Daisy asked, grabbing the remote and putting the television on pause. I turned to see her and Jordan looking at me.

"Nothing," I answered in confusion. "Why do you think something's wrong?"

"Your foot is going a mile a minute. You're also chewing on your lip. You'll be pacing next," she said ticking off each point with her fingers. "You're disturbing the show. Why are you so agitated?"

"We haven't heard anything about the case. How do you guys seem so calm?"

"We know that as soon as the others have some information for us to act on they will tell us," Daisy explained.

"We aren't the only one's working on this, Lela," Jordan added sympathetically. "We are mostly field agents. But, there are a lot more people behind the scenes here. We have to let them do their jobs and just be ready to do ours. I realize that you don't see anyone but us. You only see us because we have lots of regular human employees as well as healers and drainers. However, we generally keep the two separate for obvious reasons. We keep the humans out of danger and we don't run the risk of our secret being discovered while we are trying to do our jobs."

"And, we don't hang out with them for the same reasons. You are our only exception to that rule and you already know our secret," Daisy said.

"I heard Logan talking about teams of techs and stuff, but…I guess I didn't realize Alexander Consulting was so big," I uttered.

"We are pretty big. No doubt we will be hearing from them sooner than you think. Our people are very good at what they do. Now can we watch the rest of this now? I want to finish it before they call," Daisy pleaded.

"Sorry," I muttered. Jordan winked at me.

At ten, there was still no call, and Daisy announced that she was going home. I told her she was welcome to stay, but she said she had things to do. I suspected however, that she was leaving because of Jordan. The look he'd given her when I'd invited her to stay wasn't very welcoming. I headed for the shower and, just like the night before, when I came out Jordan was already in my bed. I crawled into the bed next to Jordan.

"You are just getting way too comfortable," I said half-heartedly. He *was* getting too comfortable. But, if I was being honest, I liked him being there. I was proud of how casual I was able to take this on the outside anyway. On the inside, I had to beat my panic down with a mental bat.

"You can always kick me out you know," he said snaking an arm around me and pulling me into the warmth of his body.

"Maybe later."

"See, progress. Now you're getting comfortable sleeping with me." His voice held a note of satisfaction.

"Sleeping is the key word here," I said firmly.

"If that's what you really want," he said in a husky voice as his fingers rubbed lightly over my belly sending little shivers over my skin. A yearning began low in my body.

"That's not going to help me go to sleep, Jordan."

"Are you ready to go to sleep now? I thought you might want to talk a little," he said sounding totally innocent.

"That's not exactly talking, either," I said starting to sound a little breathy.

"You are getting turned on just from me touching your tummy," he said clearly pleased with himself. Then he groaned, "You're so responsive you're killing me. I really wasn't trying to turn you on. Well, not really. I just like touching you."

I shoved his hand away, but he just chuckled and put it right back, continuing his stroking of my stomach.

"Tell me something," he said thoughtfully.

121

"What?"

He waited so long to speak I thought he might not say anything. "You said it had been two years since you'd dated anyone and that your relationship didn't end badly. So, what happened?"

He was referring to a conversation he'd tried to have before the whole six week disappearance.

"You seriously want to know about my previous relationship?" My voice was incredulous if not a bit surprised.

"Actually, I want to know what made you comfortable enough to have sex with whomever he was," he said a little tightly.

I turned in his arms now and looked at him. Was he serious? Yep, one look at his tight, solemn face told me he was indeed serious. He looked as if he was braced for some bad tasting medicine he was resigned to taking.

"I'm just trying to understand you, Lela." He stroked my cheek with his thumb in slow, drugging circles. "And, while the idea of someone else touching you infuriates me, there are some things I would like to know. Don't worry. I don't want details. I'm just looking for more clues to what makes you tick."

"I'm not that complicated, Jordan. I don't know exactly why I was able to…you know. I guess it just felt easy and right. I never felt out of control or all the turmoil inside that you cause me, that's for sure. I'd known him for a few years. He was a college classmate, but we'd gone to the same high school. We got to know each other, became friends and things just progressed from there. It's always been hard for me to allow people to get close to me. Hearing the thoughts of people and feeling what they feel is very difficult. It's tolerable in settings like work, where I'm distracted by other things and just don't have any intimate connections with the people around me. However, when the setting is more intimate and the focus is on a specific person, which happens when you spend time with someone, it gets weird and complicated. Most things other people think, I really don't want to know, especially when they are thinking about me."

"I guess your issues with your mother didn't make it any easier." It wasn't a question.

"No, they didn't. She was the first one whose thoughts I learned to filter out." I shivered with the memory of all of her toxic thoughts.

"You hang out with Daisy and Ethan all the time. You don't seem to have a problem with them." He sounded fascinated.

"Yes, well, I don't generally find myself in bed with them either nor kissing them. And, honestly, your minds seem to be much more settled and less random than regular people. You don't shout your feelings and thoughts at me."

"So, you're able to block out our emotions and thoughts easier?"

"Well, yes," I said thoughtfully. "I feel about as normal around you guys as I do with Blake. I don't always have to be on my guard."

"Interesting. I take it this guy's mind was also..., what? Calmer or whatever?"

"Surprisingly, his mind was rather more like you and your families. He was very easy to be around."

I frowned as I thought about this, an unsettling thought coming to mind.

"Do you think maybe he was one of us?" Jordan asked the question I was beginning to ask myself. "Maybe a healer or a drainer?"

"I don't know, but I'm starting to wonder that myself," my frown deepened.

"Don't frown," he said, dipping his head and brushing his lips across my eyebrows. "Then why did you two break up?"

I didn't realize my senses were opening until I began to feel the earnestness of his desire to understand. This need to understand me he seemed to have disarmed me. He didn't just want me, he seemed to need me. He wasn't doing anything outwardly to show what he was feeling, but I could feel his need. And, his need for me was rapidly becoming my need for him. I knew I should have closed off my senses, but his need for me was so strong and pure, I felt caught in it.

"He wanted more than I could give," I said softly, staring into his eyes.

"What does that mean?" he asked, frustration clearly in his voice.

I closed my eyes and my senses so I could think. I couldn't think while he looked at me the way he was looking at me now. I was drowning in this pool of need we were creating. I tried to slow my pounding heart and focus. When I opened my eyes again he was waiting patiently.

"So what did this other boyfriend want that you couldn't give him? If you felt comfortable enough to have sex with him then, what more could there be?"

"Geeze, you're blunt," I said feeling exposed. "He wanted more time. He was getting too serious."

I was hedging and he knew it.

"Tell me why you broke up," he insisted.

He continued to brush his lips across my face and along my jaw. I answered him in a distracted voice as he made his way to my neck and began to nibble. "I...I wasn't...ready for..."

"Ready for what?" he whispered hotly in my ear and then gently sucked my earlobe between his teeth.

124

"Wasn't ready…for such… an intense relationship. He was too intense, too possessive."

"Did you love him?" he breathed hotly into my neck as his hands began to stroke my hip and he began to gently suck on my shoulder.

"I thought I did. But…not enough…to be as serious, oh," I moaned. "He wanted to marry me."

That brought him up short. He raised his head and looked at me. "Marry you? How old were you? How old was he?"

"I was twenty and not nearly ready for such a commitment," I said jolted from the abrupt ending of his seducing attentions. The startled look on his face changed to something else. Something I couldn't identify flickered there. Before, I could ask or simply open my senses to check he took my mouth in a hot, deep kiss and all thoughts were lost.

Jordan's hands wondered languidly and expertly over my body, leaving a trail of heat. He pulled me tighter against him as his mouth slowly nibbled and sucked its way from my neck down to the tops of my breasts. My heart was pounding as my breath hitched each time he gently stroked my sensitive skin. I was going up in flames. Jordan took his time and made sure every sensitive place he touched was screaming for attention before he moved on. He'd moved a hand up under my shirt which exposed both of my breasts. My self-control was in tatters and, if I didn't put an end to this soon, I would be past the point of no return. Only, I couldn't hold on to a thought long enough to express it. The only thing I expressed was a choked groan as he kneaded and softly squeezed one breast and bent his head to nibble on the other. I arched off the bed as he covered my nipple with his lips and gradually sucked it into his mouth.

"God, you're beautiful," he murmured against my breast before turning his attention to the underside. I was gasping and writhing now

125

under his expert ministration. There was no more thought just feeling, and desire, and need as his mouth made its way to my stomach and one hand made small circles on my inner thigh.

"Tell me you want me," he whispered against my navel as he slid a finger along the heat between my legs. I was hot and wet and thought I would lose my mind as his fingers slid expertly through the liquid heat there.

"I don't," I gasped unable to complete my sentence.

"Yes, you do," he breathed against my hip and bit me lightly. "But, I won't give it to you until you tell me."

"I don't... have any... condoms," I choked out just as he began to rub between my thighs in a way that had my hips lifting off the bed. My eyes rolled back in my head. He paused and I was momentarily left panting and gasping as he made his way back up my body and looked into my eyes.

"I didn't mean - ," he began seeming surprised as he stared down at me with passion filled eyes. He swallowed hard and began again, "I mean, are you sure?"

Now I was confused. I frowned in confusion and he groaned and closed his eyes. He reached up to put a hand over mine on his chest. I'd been absentmindedly fondling his nipple.

"Oh, hell. Please tell me you are ready for this," he groaned and buried his face in my neck. "I was trying to give you time but, Baby, I need you."

"I'm ready," I was practically begging. "I just don't have any condoms."

In one smooth, unbelievably fast motion he'd rolled away and come back up with a string of condoms. Somewhere in my mind I'd have

126

to ponder how he came to have a string of condoms beside my bed. However, currently, all of my attention was on his naked chest and hard body beside me. In another of his impossibly fast movements he'd removed his already unbuttoned shirt and pajama pants. And then he began the exquisite torture again. He kissed, licked and rubbed all over my body, driving me out of my mind as he removed my pajamas.

When Jordan finally positioned himself between my thighs and slid inside with excruciating slowness, little tingly explosives seemed to go off all over my body. And then the real torture began. He set a maddeningly measured and leisure pace that had me moaning, groaning, thrashing, and pleading. It went on for what seemed like forever.

"Shh. Just relax, Lela, and let me love you," he murmured against my mouth. Just when I thought I couldn't take anymore he sent me flying over the edge. He gritted his teeth but he didn't increase the pace.

With the force of my release I started to panic at his relentless, steady rhythm. He'd been building me up for so long, I didn't think I could go on any longer. But, his masterful hands, hot mouth, and long deep strokes had me building quickly all over again. I felt spent yet my body was reacting in answer to his every demand.

"Jordan," I panted in alarm.

"One more, Lela. You've got one more for me, don't you love?" he crooned passionately.

It ended up being two more before Jordan finally succumbed with a deep guttural growl. The man was a machine and I was now as limp as a dishrag. I was already drifting to sleep when Jordan slid from my body and rolled to his side. He pulled me against him and I slept like the dead.

Chapter 19

The next time I surfaced back to the land of the living, Jordan was gently shaking me awake. It was very dark now and only the light from the yard lamps filtering through the windows was visible.

"Lela, Sweetheart, you have to wake up. Your brother is here."

My brother! Blake! I jolted up and noticed that Jordan was fully dressed. "Blake is here? Where?"

"He just pulled into the driveway. And since my car is in the drive there's no way to hide the fact that I'm here, but I didn't think you'd want him to find me in bed with you," he whispered. "He'll be inside any minute. I'm going to go lay on the sofa. You'd better figure out what you want to tell him."

This was just great. I scrambled out of bed and began looking around furiously for my pajamas.

"Your pajamas are on the night table next to the bed," he said quietly as he walked swiftly out of the room.

I quickly put my tank top and pajama pants on and slid back into bed. I felt like I was a teenager who'd been caught by my parents with a boy in my room. Yes, I was a grown woman and he was my brother, not my parent. But, he was my big brother! Though I knew Blake didn't lack for female companionship he was always very discrete. I never saw any of them since he'd stopped dating. Women found his constant traveling too hard to deal with. I was pretty sure he was only dealing with the friends with benefits type of women.

Though Blake stopped scaring away guys after I graduated from high school, I had no doubt that Blake coming home to find his sister naked and in bed with someone would not only be awkward for both of us, but upsetting to him. I'm sure he assumed that I had sex, but what big

128

brother wanted proof? I certainly didn't want to know about his sexual exploits.

I lay there waiting to hear him come in. He didn't come through the front door but through the garage. I heard the door to the laundry room open. That meant he would miss Jordan on the sofa.

He entered the house through the laundry room but didn't turn on any lights. I wondered what my hair looked like after Jordan's lovemaking, and began to run my hands over it to tame my wild curls, as I heard Blake's cautious footsteps coming down the hall. They slowed as they came to my open doorway. He had to pass my room to get to his. He halted just before he got to my door as if listening. After a moment he began to walk swiftly and quietly past my door.

"Blake?" I called out quietly.

The footsteps halted. There was some rustling as he changed directions and then his form appeared in the darkened doorway. I switched on my bedside lamp and noticed he gave my bed a quick scan before looking back at me. Relief seemed to spread through his taught features. He'd been afraid of what he might see.

"I thought I heard you come in," I smiled at him.

"I'm sorry. I didn't mean to wake you."

"That's ok. I thought you were coming home tomorrow?"

"I didn't want to spend another night in a hotel. So, I caught the last flight here tonight instead of waiting and catching my morning flight." He placed the luggage he'd been holding down on the floor by his feet. "Is that Jordan's car in the driveway?"

"Yes, he's in the living room."

He raised a brow, "Why is he in the living room?"

"I'm helping them with a case and am on call. If something happens then we'll have to leave immediately."

"What type of situation could they have with their animals that he needs to be here alone with you at night?" His voice was definitely suspicious. And, though he tried not to let it, his big brother tone was coming through. "Do, they have a sick animal or something? And if that's the case, why didn't they just have you stay there if they needed you on hand or send Daisy to stay with you?"

"No, Blake, they don't have a sick animal. This is a case their security firm is handling. I'm helping with the investigation."

Blake knew about their security and investigative business.

"How can you help them with that?" He now looked thoroughly confused.

I didn't want to keep my secret from Blake anymore. I didn't want to lie to my brother. The whole Alexander clan knew about my gift, but the person nearest and dearest to me didn't. I'd always known to keep it a secret. My grandmother had known. She'd been the one to tell me when I was a little girl to never tell anyone and never let anyone find out. I'd tried to bury it for the most part until the fateful day I'd seen Ethan get shot in the woods. Otherwise, I probably would have told Blake earlier. I looked up to see him scrutinizing me. He seemed to be seeing far more than I wanted him to, but I wasn't sure just what that was.

"Blake, I need to tell you something that I probably should have told you a long time ago," I began. His eyes stopped roaming suspiciously over me and my bed and his eyes sharpened on my face. "It turns out, I have something that the Alexanders found useful to this investigation."

He stiffened, and his voice came out hushed, "Are you talking about your ability to read people, or their minds, or whatever?"

130

I stared at him open mouthed.

"You knew?" I breathed.

"Well, I knew you could when you were a child. Granny could do it too. She told me to never speak of it and look out for you so that no one would find out," he whispered. "Are you telling me you told them about it?"

"Well, yes, I guess I did?" I muttered still shocked that he'd known all this time.

"Why would you do that, Lela?" His voice held reproach and a hint of panic. "It's dangerous for people to know that. And now they're trying to exploit you?"

"No. They aren't, Blake," I said putting a hand up to stop his protest. "They've known for a while. Actually, Daisy kind of figured it out. It was totally my decision to help with this current case."

"I didn't even know if you could still do it. How did Daisy figure it out?" he asked puzzled.

"When I tried to, well, listen to her mind, she felt it."

"Felt it?" His frown deepened. "How?"

"I don't know. She just knew I was trying to read her." I shrugged. He became thoughtful.

"So, you are using your gift to help them with a case, and that is why Jordan is here with you, alone at night?" he clarified, still sounding unconvinced. His eyes flickered across my blanket covered body again and back to my face. My upper half was exposed and, even though I had my pajama tank top on, I was starting to feel like I should pull my sheet up to my chin.

"Yes. It's a kidnapping case, and they are having me sit in on interrogations. I'm not sure I'm even supposed to tell you that. But, if we get a call on a lead we are waiting for, we will have to leave right away."

"Uh, huh," he said noncommittally, his eyes flickering over me again. "Well, then I guess you'd better get some rest then. I'm headed to bed. I'm tired."

He bent down, lifted his suitcase and walked down the hall to his room without another word. Moments later I heard his door close, which was odd because we never slept with our doors closed. He was upset. But why? I was so tempted to open my senses and see just what he was thinking. I didn't hear him coming but, a few seconds after Blake's door closed, Jordan was standing in my doorway. He came in and closed the door silently.

"Well, that went well, I guess," I said feeling frazzled. "He seemed to believe me, yet he still seemed upset. It was like he was biting his tongue or something."

"You didn't read his mind?" Jordan asked, amusement and a twinge of concern lit his eyes.

"No. I keep telling you I don't just go around listening to people's thoughts," I grumbled.

"You are a better person than me, but I'm pretty sure I know what he's thinking."

He was eyeing me in a way that had dread rising in my chest.

"How would you know?" I asked cautiously.

"Well, you have these red marks on your shoulders and the base of your throat that could be easily covered with a t-shirt. But, in that tank top, they look suspiciously like hickeys," he said evenly as if he wasn't the culprit.

132

"Hickeys!" I hissed. "You left hickeys on me?"

I jumped out of bed and over to my mirror. Sure enough, there were suspicious red marks on both of my shoulders and one right in the v of my cleavage. I groaned, putting a hand over my face in disgust. I felt Jordan drift towards me and stand behind me. He placed both of his hands on my shoulders.

"I'm sorry," he said in my hair. "Don't be upset. It will be ok."

"Jordan, he knows what we've been doing," I whined with embarrassment.

"Yes he does," he stated calmly. "Are you afraid he's going to be angry with you?"

"No. Not angry," I thought. "Well, maybe a little."

"Lela, you're a grown woman," he reasoned.

"Yes, but, he's still my big brother." I turned around to face him and he dropped his hands from my shoulders. "This has to be a big brother nightmare."

"I'm sure he's not exactly happy about it, but I doubt it's a nightmare," he drawled. "You're over reacting. If he were that over protective he'd probably have pummeled me on the sofa by now. Get some sleep and we'll deal with it together tomorrow."

"And, what would you have done if he did?" I asked curiously.

"Did what?"

"Pummeled you."

"I would have let him," he shrugged. "It's not like he can really hurt me. And after all, I was the one who left the hickeys on his little sister. Now go to sleep."

He turned me towards the bed and nudged me towards it. I crawled back in and buried myself under the light summer weight blanket.

133

Jordan was right. I would deal with this tomorrow. I would bury myself under my covers and hide for now. I was probably over reacting a little but it didn't make me feel any less embarrassed and self-conscious. I didn't even have time to contemplate how I felt about what happened between us before I had to wonder what my brother thought about it. How could I sleep now?

Chapter 20

"What are you thinking about?" Jordan asked placing a hand over mine as he drove us to whatever location Logan had alerted him to. After the hickey incident, I must have fallen asleep as soon as Jordan left my room. It had felt like I'd just fallen asleep when Jordan was back, shaking me gently awake again. In fact it was three in the morning. The hickey incident with Blake had happened around midnight.

Jordan had gotten a call from Logan and it was time to go to work. I had been in desperate need of a shower though. I'd fallen asleep after Jordan had made love to me without one. I'd felt sticky and weird. Jordan had already taken one while I was sleeping apparently. But, the way he kept sniffing me, I was worried that I hadn't washed nearly good enough.

"I was just thinking about last night," I said distractedly.

"So was I." His voice took on a wicked, sensual tone. "That was so hot."

"I was actually thinking about my brother and the hickeys," I retorted sardonically.

"I'm sorry." He didn't sound sorry at all. "But, you don't really think he's going to give you a hard time do you? I mean what's he going to do, put you on a time out?"

134

"No, he won't give me a hard time. It's just…I don't know, awkward. I don't know how to explain it. He's my big brother. The one who always intimidated all the guys in school who showed an interest. He doesn't bring women home, at least not overnight. And, I'm the one who gets caught, with hickeys to add just a little more embarrassment to it."

"So, you didn't want your brother to know about us?" he asked quietly.

"I don't care if he knows we are involved. But he doesn't need to know what we do and when. Do you really want to know when your brother and Grace are having sex?"

"Well, no. But, I think I'd want to know even less when Daisy does. She's like a sister to me. I see your point."

"How far away is this place anyway?" I asked, deliberately changing the subject.

"Quite a ways actually. It's about forty five minutes away. We should be there in about twenty more minutes. Two other operatives are waiting on us. Logan wants us to call as soon as we know who is in there. He thinks this may be the place. It's remote and actually owned by the guy Kevin says is trying to frame him. It's late and everyone may be asleep. Can you pick up on sleeping minds?"

"I don't know. I've never tried."

"I guess we'll find out when we get there. So, you are ok with everyone knowing about us right?" He asked, returning to the topic I'd just tried to change.

"Well, we don't need to broadcast it," I said squirming. "I mean, it's not a big secret, but we don't have to go announcing it."

"Hmm," he said giving me a glance I couldn't quite read.

"What?"

"Nothing," he shook his head. "And, what about us? Are we ok?"

"Yes. Why wouldn't we be?" I asked looking out of the window.

"Because, I'm sure you are overthinking what we did last night. And, I'm not sure you know yet how you feel about it. However, the fact that you can't look at me right now makes me think it's not sitting well with you."

"Jordan, please don't start analyzing me."

"I'm not trying to analyze you. I'm trying to keep you from over analyzing," he said pointedly. "I know you. And before you start backing away and letting your mind run away with you I want to stop it. If you would stop over thinking everything and just go with it, I think we can make this work."

I said nothing, just continued starring out the window. Jordan thankfully didn't say anything else either. So we rode in silence along the dark highway.

Twenty minutes later we pulled into a short drive that led to a modest farmhouse that looked as though it had seen better days. Some of the windows were boarded up and it had a look of disrepair. Though there was no resemblance, something about it reminded me of the barnlike structure I'd been taken to when Kevin's crew had kidnapped me. Perhaps it was the remoteness of the place. Whatever it was that conjured up the memories, it sent an involuntary shudder through me. Jordan looked at me sharply but turned away just as a large figure appeared at his window. I jumped and stifled a scream. Two pairs of startled eyes turned to me. Jordan was rolling down his window when I recognized the figure at the window.

"Shane?" My voice was full of disbelief. What the heck was he doing here?

"Hi, Lela," he grinned as Jordan released the door locks and Shane climbed in the backseat. His easy smile took on a surprised look as he glanced quickly between Jordan and me. Then his face went blank as he slid across the back seat.

"Hey, Lela," Beto smiled, climbing in after Shane. Beto also seemed to be surprised and shot a look between Jordan and me. Then his face broke out in a grin as he looked away. I'd turned around to stare at them and turned back around to see Jordan watching me with an unreadable expression. Ok, this night, or early morning as it was now, was stranger and stranger by the hour. What was with the weird glances?

"How many people are in the house that you know of?" Jordan directed his attention to the backseat.

"There are six guards we know of. Three inside and three outside. They've been rotating. However, there could be more inside we don't know about. With the television on and all the movement inside it's hard to be sure. According to the surveillance team that located the place, several people were in and out of here today. But, only one drainer, a man, came earlier but left after less than an hour," Beto answered.

"They are guarding something," Shane chimed in. "We're just not sure what. Logan told us to wait for you to see if we could confirm if Mr. Beck was in there or not. He says we don't want them to know how much we are finding out about their organization until we get Mr. Beck out safely."

"Yes. Mr. Beck is the priority," Jordan agreed.

"Can you get anything, Lela?" He turned to me now and he was all business, completely focused on the task at hand.

I closed my eyes and opened my senses, concentrating on the little house. At first I just picked up a mass of disjointed chaos with fragmented words. This was what I normally got when I inadvertently or purposely opened my senses in an area with people around. I knew I'd be able to sense if people were around, but I'd never tried to isolate any one mind like this before. Usually I was focusing directly where the person I was trying to read was, like I did with Kevin in the interrogation room, if not looking directly at them as I had that day in the conference room when Daisy discovered my ability.

The noise in my head sounded more like the tuning of a radio when someone is searching for a specific station, bits and pieces of different songs and words and the white noise in between. I began trying to sift through the noise and focus on just one thing at a time. Someone was thinking about food and sleep. I held my focus there and began to feel fatigue and boredom. One of the guards maybe? I tried to relax into the drifting current of this mind. His mind flitted from one thing to another in a lazy random way. He was simply bored with nothing to do or think about. Images began to flow through my mind. An image of a porch light at the door was coupled with a desire to go inside.

"Guard at one o'clock by the front porch?" I wasn't sure if he was at that location, but that's how it looked based on the image I could see.

"Can she see that?" Beto's astonished voice whispered from the backseat.

I opened my eyes to see Jordan smiling at me and looking pleased. "Very nice. We can actually see him though. Anything else?"

"I know there are more people. I just have to try to isolate them individually," I said closing my eyes again. I picked up another thought from the random chaos emitting from the house and realized someone was inside the house watching television. They were amused at some comedy show. I could actually pick up a lot of the crude comedian's jokes as they

138

filtered through the man's mind and he reacted to them. I wondered belatedly how I knew it was a man as I withdrew from his mind. I don't know how, but I knew it was a man and his mind was more disturbing. There was a sense of callousness about him and meanness.

"There's a man inside watching some sort of comedy show," I said to no one in particular.

"How is she doing that?" Beto asked, the excitement coming off of him distracting my concentration.

"How indeed," Shane muttered completely mesmerized.

I remembered then that Shane and Beto didn't know about my gift. I wasn't sure I wanted anyone else to know, but I couldn't dwell on that right now. I opened my eyes and shook my head to clear it. "Beto, I'm going to need you to tone down the fascination. You're distracting my concentration."

"But how - " Beto began.

"Later, Beto," Jordan said through gritted teeth.

"Right. Ok. Later," he said and refocused his attention on the house. The feeling of excitement in the car dropped dramatically. I could feel Shane pondering me also, but he kept it in check and focused most of his attention on the house.

I returned my concentration back to the house and was eventually able to isolate three more people with very erratic thoughts and feelings on the inside. As I focused on each one in turn, I realized they were in different stages of sleep. Two had very erratic yet active minds while the other was more agitated and not so random. I felt fear strongly in this mind. Even in sleep the mind had a constant feeling of fear with flashes of anger, anxiety and helplessness.

"There's a fourth person in there," I blurted out. "There are three inside sleeping. Two with very erratic thoughts and feelings as though dreaming. I think the other is also sleeping, but he's not so erratic. Even in sleep I get a sense of fear and anxiety among other things."

"Anybody in there we need to worry about?" Jordan asked.

"Nope. Just regular humans," Shane replied. "We only smelled one drainer. We think he was the one the scouts reported that came and left before we got to the scene."

"Wait, if you can smell the people in there then, why do you need me?" I asked, trying not to be weirded out by the idea that they could smell people. Heck, they could smell me. What did I smell like? Shane continued, cutting off my line of thinking.

"There have been several people here today," Shane explained. "The different smells all together make it difficult to tell who is here and who isn't. Some of the fainter smells would indicate that the individual that smell belongs to has been gone longer. Or, it could mean that the person is in the house and hasn't come out for a long while. Just like any other smell, they linger inside longer even if the person is no longer there but goes away faster outside. As we haven't been in the house yet, we don't know who's in there."

"Oh," I said blankly. I was confused. "So, wait, you guys can smell them too?"

"Beto is a drainer and Shane is half healer," Jordan explained quickly and then continued, "So, if there are three inside sleeping, and one is possibly Mr. Beck, plus one inside watching television, and one outside, that equals five. If there are six guards then we are missing two."

What? Shane was a healer? Or, rather half healer? And, Beto was a drainer? I guess that would explain why Beto had been around so much

140

when I was sequestered at the ranch before. I had somehow assumed only the Alexander family were the super humans. And Shane? Here I had been contemplating having a normal chance at a relationship with Shane and he was half healer?

"They are around the other side of the house," Shane answered.

"So, that means there is definitely a seventh person here that is unaccounted for," Jordan said, looked at me and frowned. "You ok?"

I nodded and he put his hand over mine and gently squeezed. I refocused. I couldn't get lost in this new tangent. He released my hand, pulled out his phone and did some rapid tapping.

"I sent Logan a text to let him know that we think we've got Mr. Beck. Do you think you can listen in and confirm it?" Jordan inquired, looking at me hopefully. "Once we storm this place, the alarm will be sounded that we're on to them."

"I can try."

Jordan's phone beeped. He glanced at it briefly and then slid it back into his pocket.

"Logan says he already has a team headed our way. He doesn't want us to move until they get here but, in the meantime, hopes we can confirm Mr. Beck's presence."

For some reason, the news that Logan had backup coming our way, made me feel much better. Not that I didn't think my current companions could keep me safe, but we were so far away that if anything happened to any of us, help would be a long time coming.

"Maybe you can do that thing you did with Ethan and Logan in the interrogation room," Jordan suggested, sending the thoughts directly into my mind.

141

"That would probably completely freak Mr. Beck out. Besides, I'd rather not broadcast it," I disagreed back to his mind. Then I spoke out loud. "Let me see what I can do."

I closed my eyes again and searched for the fearful sleeper. I located him easier this time. I got a feeling of cold fear, confusion and dread. He wasn't in a deep sleep at all. I pondered how I could possibly wake him up without speaking directly to him when the image of his wife came to mind. When I'd met her that first time at the beginning of the investigation, she'd been worried and stressed. She'd explained how she'd waken up to find him gone. I began replaying the whole scene back and thinking it to him. He reacted immediately. After just a moment his mind seemed to jerk into consciousness and her name popped into his head. I don't know if he spoke it out loud or just thought it, but it was loud and clear in my mind. His mind began to fill with images of his wife and children.

"It's him," I breathed, not realizing I'd been holding my breath as I felt his anguish and pain.

"You're sure?" Jordan asked.

"Yes," I answered trying to calm my panicked breathing. My body was reacting to Mr. Beck's anxiety. I began talking in Jordan's head. For some reason, I didn't want Beto and Shane to know everything I could do. *"I started replaying our meeting with his wife to him and he jolted awake. Then I started to see images of his wife and kids in his head. I didn't send any thoughts of his kids."*

"Are you ok?" He looked down at me with a worried frown.

"I'm fine," I said, taking a deep breath to calm my heartbeat. It was still racing from feeling Mr. Beck's strong emotions.

142

"Ok, then. I'll let Logan know. Then we'll wait for the cavalry to arrive so we can go in and get him out of there," Jordan said picking up his phone and typing a text to Logan. Just as he put his phone down, all three of their heads whipped around to the road behind us. I turned too in confusion, wondering what had grabbed all of their attention.

Chapter 21

"Shit," Beto swore. "We've got company and it's not just the regular guys this time."

"I hope the cavalry gets here soon, but we can't wait. Shane, you take out the people in the house," Jordan ordered quickly as he shot off another text to Logan. "Leave Mr. Beck inside until all is clear. You can work your way back to us after the house is secured. We'll hold them off. Make it fast Shane. As soon as the house is clear come back and lock Lela in there too. I want her out of the way before the fighting starts."

"Then you'd better send her with me now," Shane said gravely slipping soundlessly out of the car, "because, they are already here."

"It's too dangerous," Jordan snarled in frustration.

"Shane should lock himself in the house with me. He can't fight these drainers," I said fearing for Shane's safety. He was only half healer. Surely a half healer couldn't take on these full blooded drainers.

Jordan shot me a steely look that froze me where I sat. "Shane is half healer. He'll be fine."

Half healer. But didn't that mean he only had half the strength as a regular healer?

"She can hold her own with regular humans, Jordan, much better than she could with drainers," Shane countered urgently.

"He's right, Jordan," Beto agreed.

"Fine. Go! Go now!" Jordan barked as headlights began to appear behind us.

Shane jerked me unceremoniously out of the car and headed for the dilapidated house. Running as fast as I could, I was still stumbling behind him. As we made our way from the road and to the porch the cars pulled into the yard. He never let go of my arm and never let me fall, he just dragged me along. Faster than it seemed possible we were at the house and he released me. I staggered onto the porch just as he flew to the side and, with a few deft moves, had the guard that had been bored outside slumped in his arms. The door flew open and I turned to look into the face of the man who I knew had been watching television. For some reason I knew it was him even though I'd never seen his face before. He glanced at me and grinned just as someone stepped up behind him. He glanced to the side and frowned as he saw Shane propping the guard against the wall. He grabbed me as the other man behind him took in the scene and reached for his gun.

I broke his hold and delivered a few swift blows. The man went down just as Shane disarmed the man with the gun. He was putting the second man next to the first when the big man I'd knocked down to the ground came after me again.

"You wanna take me on you little bitch?" he roared and lunged at me. I twisted as he lunged, grabbing him and flinging him to the ground. I delivered a few precise blows and he was rolling around in a ball on the ground.

"I've got your bitch," I spat out and then landed another blow that knocked him out cold.

"Not bad," I heard Shane's amused voice behind me. "Not bad at all."

I looked up and saw him grinning at me like a proud Papa.

"Why is it that the first thing men do is call a woman a bitch when they get mad? Is that like the go to word?" I huffed. "It's getting a little tired."

I kicked the man lightly again for good measure as I stood up from my kneeling position. Then, we heard footsteps running from the side of the house and inside the house. All hell broke loose as people exploded from cars, the side of the house and inside the house. Some of them moved so fast I couldn't see them. They literally blurred. Shane, Beto and Jordan were blurring in a half circle around the porch with several other people and I was in the middle.

"Lela, behind you!" Shane was shouting. I swung around to see the two guards who'd come from around the side of the house. They were standing there in different states of confusion before finally focusing on me. They looked as if they weren't sure what to do with me until they looked down at their fallen comrade I was standing over. Then, it was on.

I'd never fought more than one person at a time before, well, at least not outside of black belt training. But, that was just sparring. Still, I prepared myself just as I would in class. They attacked simultaneously from different sides. I side stepped while delivering a strike to one guys gut. The other did manage to catch me in the chest and, though my momentum didn't allow him to get a good grip, it sent me sprawling. I rolled and was back on my feet. The guy who'd hit me rushed me now, punching. I blocked, grabbed his arm and just as I was about to break it and flip him I was grabbed from behind by the man I'd gotten in the gut. I didn't let go of the first man's bent arm however. As the creep behind me grabbed me around the neck and lifted me in a headlock, I jerked the other man's arm up with me and heard a satisfying crunch as I brought my leg

145

up to deliver a kick to his bent over solar plexus. Still choking I brought my elbow back into my chokers gut, and as his grip loosened slightly I did a break away move and caught his thumb and tried to rip the damn thing off. He released me fully then, and I went to work on him running on pure adrenaline.

"Well done," came a familiar voice behind me. I spun around to see Shane striding towards me. He was grinning from ear to ear like an idiot. "I'd better get you inside."

"No, I can help," I protested. "I can take out more of the regular people."

"Yes, well, I'm sure you could. You seem to be enjoying this a bit too much," he said with slight amusement before glancing anxiously at the road. "But, from the sounds coming from the road, I'd better get you inside. Jordan would kill me if something happened to you."

He pulled me inside the open door, closed, and locked it.

"Stop right there," came a deadly calm voice from the darkened hall. The sixth guard. I'd forgotten about the sixth man and apparently so had Shane. I'd figured he had come out of the house and was part of the melee outside. Shane immediate halted and put his hands in the air. The man cautiously stepped out of the hallway where he was holding a shotgun.

"Move away from the door," he ordered and gestured with the gun where he wanted us to move. We moved. We couldn't let the man move to the door, but I was at a loss as to how to stop him. This wasn't the time to be respectful or modest so I opened my senses to see if Shane had a plan. I could feel Shane's mind thinking around for a solution. He thought he could take the man but was afraid if he shot the gun he might actually hit me. He was trying to think of a way to focus the man's attention on

146

him. Doing so, however, increased his chances of getting shot. I could feel his decision solidifying in his mind. He was going to make himself a target and hope for the best.

In complete panic and desperation an image came to me from nowhere. I imagined the most grotesque face from a horror movie that I could think of standing in the doorway behind the man. I threw the image at his mind with a screech from the depths of hell. The man swung around and began shooting. In a flash, Shane was on the terrified man. Maybe my regular eyes couldn't tell, but Shane seemed to move just as quickly as the rest of the super humans. One minute the guy was shooting down the hall and the next he was slumped over and being placed against the wall.

"Why did you scream?" Shane demanded, looking at me quizzically, as he was tying the man's arms with his own belt and propping him against the wall.

Realizing that I had screamed out loud when I threw the image at this last man's mind, I searched for some explanation. "I wanted him to think there was something behind him."

That was at least mostly true. It seemed to satisfy Shane anyway.

"Let's go check on Mr. Beck." He gestured to the hall. We walked down the hall to the only closed door there was. It was locked. Shane made short work of the lock, further surprising me. Apparently locks were no big deterrent for him either. He swung the door open cautiously to reveal a much shaken Mr. Beck huddled in the corner. He'd probably hit the floor when he heard the gunshots.

Mr. Beck was a tall, athletically built man who looked like he'd seen better days. He was rumpled and dirty but appeared ready to fight when Shane and I burst through the door. He stood abruptly then paused, looking confused when he saw me. I spoke quickly to try and put him at ease. I didn't want to have to tie him up too.

"Mr. Beck. We are here to get you out of here," I spoke rapidly. "However, the house is being attacked right now by the people who kidnapped you. Once we get them under control we will be taking you away from here."

"What? Who are you? Why would the people who kidnapped me be attacking the house?" he asked skeptically. I already had my senses open from trying to locate him in the house and dealing with the last guard. I could feel that he wanted to believe me but didn't want to fall for a trick either.

"Well, uh, we are from Alexander Consulting and Security. Your wife hired us to find you," I said trying to sound reassuring. "They are attacking because they are trying to prevent us from rescuing you."

"What's going on out there?" he asked, still keeping his distance from us and still in a fright.

"Like I said, the house is under attack right now," I stated calmly. "Our, uh, extraction team is fighting with your kidnappers right now. So, we have to stay put until they can secure the area."

"And, I need to get out there and help," Shane added gravely. He was clearly beginning to lose patience. He gave Mr. Beck a hard stare. "This is Lela. She's here to help you. I know you've been through a lot and don't know what to think or who to trust. Unfortunately, we don't have time to give you all the assurances you need if we are going to get you out of here, and ourselves, unharmed. But, know this. If you touch her, or try to hurt her in any way, you die."

Mr. Beck's eyes widened. He stared back at Shane's stern face and then at me. He had no intention of coming near me as long as I didn't come after him. He was hoping to heaven we were telling him the truth.

"Now stay inside and stay down just in case bullets start flying again. Don't let anyone in here. If anyone gets in, do your best to take them out," Shane commanded and then was out the door.

I turned to see that, Mr. Beck was in the same spot, huddled in the far corner. I closed and relocked the bedroom door from the inside. Mr. Beck glanced at me warily. For a moment we both just stood there listening to the raging battle outside. It sounded like Armageddon out there. There were crashes, thuds, yelling and things smashing.

"Your wife and children are so worried about you," I said trying to distract us both with conversation. "They will be so happy to have you home."

"You've seen my wife? My kids?" he asked, something breaking inside of him. "Are they ok?"

"Other than being worried sick over you, they are just fine," I reassured him with a smile. "They've been under our protection since your wife called us in on the case."

"I don't understand what all of this is about," he said, his voice full of frustrated confusion.

I wasn't sure what I should tell him. After all, I was just helping with the case. But, I felt like I needed to tell him something. I approached him slowly and he didn't tense or flinch.

"Well, I can't say I know all of the details. I'm sure, Logan, the leader on the case, will be able to give you more details. All I really know is that you were kidnapped for ransom and we needed to find you."

"Ransom? Who would want to kidnap me?"

Again, not knowing what the official story would be, I didn't want to say any more than I already had. "I'm sorry I don't have more information for you. But, I can assure you, someone will be giving you all of the information you want when this is all over. I'm only part of the rescue team."

Thankfully after what seemed like forever, the battle outside seemed to come to a sudden halt. I'd been trying not to worry about Jordan, Beto, and Shane. I was pretty sure they were outnumbered. Shane had told Jordan that I would do better against the humans than the drainers that were arriving. But, I had no way of knowing how many drainers there were or how they were fairing. What if they were overrun? I didn't even have a weapon. Mr. Beck and I would be sitting ducks.

From beyond the door of the room we were holed up in, we could hear the front door open. Mr. Beck and I both stared at the door. No one called out, and I was beginning to fear that maybe Jordan, Beto, and Shane had been overrun. Belatedly I opened my senses to see if I could determine friend or foe and was surprised to feel Ethan's mind. I slumped against the wall with relief. He was being stealthy just in case someone had gotten past them and made it into the house.

"We're down the hall and to the right," I thought to his mind. I could feel his mind relax a little with the knowledge that I was alright. *"You scared the hell out of me. Why didn't you say something?"*

"I didn't want you to call out and give your location away just in case someone got past us," he thought back.

"Why didn't you think something to me?"

"Oh. Well, I didn't think about it. I keep forgetting that's an option with you."

I could feel his grin as I heard his gentle knock on the door.

"Who's there?" I asked cautiously for Mr. Beck's sake. Obviously I knew it was Ethan.

"It's me, Ethan," Ethan answered sounding incredulous, not considering the fact that Mr. Beck was not privy to my ability or our mental conversation. "Open up."

Mr. Beck stiffened.

"It's ok. He's one of the good guys," I reassured him and opened the locked bedroom door.

Ethan stepped in and began looking me over critically. He also did the little sniffing the air thing Beto had done. "You ok? Shane said you had to do some fighting too?"

"I'm fine."

Seemingly satisfied after a quick once over, he introduced himself to Mr. Beck and hustled us out of there. Logan and Daisy met us at the front door. I noticed they also did the sniff thing only, Daisy smiled and Logan gave Jordan a hard glance.

Jordan was making his way towards us looking a little worse for wear. Beto and Shane were also standing at the base of the stairs looking like they too had gotten a run for their money in the battle. My concern must have been plain on my face.

"You should see the other guys," Beto grinned, and then cursed as his split lip split even further.

"You ok?" Jordan asked, coming to stand in front of me and looking me over for injuries. He frowned at my neck.

"Better than you, I think. Are you alright?" I asked checking out his cuts and bruises.

"I'm fine," he said waving away my question and pulling me to him. He lifted my face, inspecting it and then gently touched my neck. I winced. It hurt. Jordan's eyes became stormy.

"I'm fine, Jordan. Really," I said sternly. He looked as if he was going to say something but Logan put a hand on his shoulder and squeezed briefly. Then, Logan stepped over to Mr. Beck, introduced himself and took charge of him.

"Mr. Beck, we are waiting for word from our team protecting your wife that your house is secure," he was saying.

"My wife? Is she safe?" he sounded panicked.

"Yes. She is perfectly safe. However, some of the people who kidnapped you were keeping watch on your wife and your home. Our people are aware of them but didn't want to let on that we were until you were safe. Your wife and children have been under our protection since she first called us into this case."

"Can I talk to her? Can I call her?" he asked growing agitated.

"We expect the all clear any moment now. As soon as we got the confirmation that you were here, the order was given to round up those watching your home. They will allow her to call as soon as there is no longer a threat around your home," Logan assured him. "Now, however, we need to get you out of here just in case reinforcements are on their way."

Logan turned to the operatives milling around and was shouting orders as he lead Mr. Beck to a waiting SUV. There were quite a number of people around and by the looks of it, most were part of Logan's crew. The ones that weren't were being cuffed, or picked up and hauled into cars. Clearly those from Kevin's organization hadn't done very well against the Alexander crew.

"Jordan, Take Lela to Grace and then home. Then you, Beto, and Shane meet me back at the Ranch. I'll be escorting Mr. Beck home as soon as we get the all clear."

Chapter 22

Jordan led me back to his car followed by Shane and Beto. As we were walking to the car, Beto sniffed the air again and grinned slyly at Jordan. Jordan ignored him. What was with the sniffing? Shane and Beto took off in whatever car they had arrived in and Jordan ushered me quickly into his SUV. I leaned my head against the window of the passenger door and alternately stared out of the window and closed my eyes. Now that the excitement was over, and I wasn't being energized by adrenaline, I was exhausted.

"Will you stay with me after you see Grace?" Jordan asked into the quietness of the car. I lifted my head and turned to him, but he continued looking straight ahead watching the road.

"I'm really tired, Jordan. And my brother is home. I haven't seen him in weeks." My voice was weary with fatigue, and I was feeling like I really needed some time alone. I felt overstimulated and needy, two things that I never dealt with well. So much had happened and I needed some time to rest and review. I also didn't think I was ready for Jordan to make a habit out of us spending every waking, or sleeping, moment together. I wasn't even sure how I felt about us making love. Jordan was right, I did want to retreat. I wasn't going back on my decision to give us a try. I just needed time to think.

"Just for a little while. We can catch a few hours of sleep and I'll take you home by noon," Jordan reasoned, interrupting my brooding thoughts. His voice was even but there was a hint of something that I couldn't name there. "Please, Lela. I need you."

"That doesn't sound like sleep is what you have in mind," I frowned.

"As much as I am dying to make love to you again, I give you my word, I only want to sleep," he assured me. "Even I have to sleep sometimes. After Grace finishes checking us over for bumps and bruises, and I get a quick shower, I'll need at least a couple of hours of sleep. I want to feel you next to me."

The thought made me shiver. I really liked feeling Jordan sleeping next to me. The fact that I did like it so much also made me feel uncomfortable. I was trying to let Jordan in but it felt more like I was being taken over.

"I don't know, Jordan," I hedged. "Besides, I need a shower too. And I don't have any clothes."

"Just sleep, Lela. And you can sleep in one of my shirts and your clothes will be washed while you're sleeping," he countered. "I know you want to pull away, Lela. I can feel it. I'm just asking for a few hours of sleep and then you go home. I'll even have Daisy take you home. I just don't want you to pull away now."

I didn't have the energy to argue with him. I was only good for sleep at the moment, and I doubted even Jordan's arsenal of sensual persuasion could change that. Besides, it was only six in the morning according to the digital clock on the dash, and I didn't want to face Blake without some rest. Just the thought of having to face Blake was enough to have me agreeing.

"Fine."

When we arrived Grace was waiting for us. Beto and Shane trailed in behind us and looked a lot better than they did when we'd left the chaos of the battle. I realized then that they were able to heal themselves. Or rather, they healed faster than a normal person. Jordan also looked better than he had, so clearly drainers could do some self-healing. But, neither he nor Beto looked as good as Shane. Shane simply looked tired. What minor cuts and bruises he'd acquired that were visible looked old.

Grace came over and began fussing over them, just as he'd said. After checking each of them over as they hit the door she instructed them to go and rest. She sniffed the air and shot a look of surprise at Jordan. She didn't say anything but simply schooled her features into a businesslike expression. She immediately went to touching him with her magical, healing hands and then turned to me. She looked at me and frowned at the bruising on my neck.

"What happened to you?" she asked, her eyes widening. She turned a glare on Jordan, Beto, and Shane.

"I'm fine, Grace," I hurried to assure her.

"Fine?" She objected in distress. "You call this fine."

She grabbed my face and gently placed her other hand on my neck. Immediately I felt the healing peppermint feeling sooth my neck.

"How did this happen?" she demanded, turning her sharpened eyes on the guys again.

"Lela took out a few bad guys while we were extracting Mr. Beck," Shane said softly and gave me a fist bump. "She kicked ass."

"Yea, you should see the other guys," Beto added. "It was pretty hot."

"Guys? How many were you fighting?" Graces eyes turned back to me, some of her anger replaced by concern.

155

"Grace, she's tired," Jordan chimed in before I could answer her. "And, I'm sure her throat hurts."

"Yes. You're right," she acquiesced reluctantly. "We can discuss it later, after you've rested."

After she finished applying her magic fingers to my neck, she ordered me to go rest as well. While Logan was off tying up loose ends and getting Mr. Beck back to his family, Grace was directing everyone's cleaning up and bedding down. She'd gathered my clothes once I was in the shower and I came out to find a nightshirt with the tags still on it on the bed.

"Grace said to tell you that this was one she'd bought but never used," Jordan said when I came out of his bathroom wrapped in a towel. He stood from the chair he'd been sitting in and headed for the shower I'd just vacated. Once I'd put lotion all over my body and then the night shirt Grace provided, I crawled into Jordan's bed. I did realize that I was breaking my own etiquette rules and thought it strange that no one seemed to care. Grace had brought a nightgown to me in Jordan's room.

Jordan came out of the bathroom a few minutes later with his pajama bottoms on and crawled into bed. I was already starting to doze.

"Hey, Jordan?" I mumbled.

"What, Babe," he said nuzzling in my hair.

"Maybe, I shouldn't be in here. I mean, I'm not sure it's appropriate for us to be sleeping in your bed together."

"It's just sleeping, Lela," he sighed.

"Yes, well, sleeping together implies that we are *sleeping* together," I said turning to him now.

156

"They already know were having sex, Lela," he mumbled sounding half sleep.

"What? How?" I asked turning in his arms now fully awake. He opened one eye and looked at me for a moment. Then, he closed his eye as if he were going to go to sleep and not answer me.

"How the hell could they know that?" I shoved him accusingly. "Who did you tell?"

"I didn't tell anyone," he said, both eyes popping open. "They can smell me on you."

"What?" I practically shouted. What the hell was that supposed to mean? "I took a shower."

"Yes, but, it was a quick one. And you didn't wash your hair. I've been smelling me on you all night and you on me. Our scents are less mingled now that we've taken a second shower though."

"The sniffing!" I said understanding now and flushing with embarrassment. "That's what all of the sniffing was about?"

"Can we talk about this in a few hours," Jordan grumbled pulling me back into his side.

"Why didn't you tell me?" I chided, ignoring his request. "And, you were in my bed, but that didn't mean we had sex. So you're saying us being here together now is going to make everyone assume we're having sex?"

Well, they'd probably assume that anyway, I thought belatedly.

"No," he sighed resignedly propping himself up on an elbow. "Sex definitely has its own smell."

"So, you just let me walk around smelling like a brothel – "

"You don't smell like a brothel. You smelled like me," he said in a garbled voice muffled by the pillow as he rolled over face first into the bed.

He growled with impatience and then rolled back up on his elbow to stare at me incredulously. "I didn't want you freaking out. We had to go."

"Seriously, how can they possibly smell…well…us?" I asked flustered. "You mean they will know every time we have sex?"

"Geeze woman! We aren't even having sex at the moment and you're still freaking out about it!" Jordan hissed. The next thing I knew, I was pulled down on my back and Jordan was hovering above me. "No, Lela. They don't have to know each time we have sex. I assume when you took a shower it was more if a rinse off?"

"Well, yes."

"Yes, well, you didn't wash my scent off of you. I had been all over you. Our sensitive noses can pick that up. And after I showered while you were sleeping, I crawled back into bed with you. The same bed we'd just made love in. Your bed is full of the scent of our lovemaking. Now, I just spent the entire night trying to ignore the lingering scent so I could focus on my job. If you don't let this go until we can get some sleep, I'm going to think you are ready for a repeat performance. Now go to sleep!"

With that, he slid off of me, pulled me into him again and threw and arm around me. I just lay there digesting what he'd just said. Moments later, I heard his breathing change. I realized dubiously that he was asleep. That was the last thought I remembered, so I must have fallen off too.

I wasn't sure what woke me up, but I snuggled closer to Jordan's warmth and tried to go back to sleep. The Sky was still dark outside when Jordan and I had first crawled into his bed, but dawn had been fast approaching. Now the sun was up and streaming through the window. I heard a light knock at the door.

"I know you hear me, Jordan. You're going to regret it if you keep ignoring everyone," Logan's voice came through the door. "I'm opening the door now."

I opened my eyes to see the door slowly opening, however, no one appeared. Logan's disembodied voice just drifted in through the open doorway. "Mom and Dad are here. So, unless you want Lela to be embarrassed by meeting them in bed with you, I suggest you get up now."

"What?" I asked sitting straight up as Jordan groaned.

"You've got about five minutes before they hit the front door." With that, he closed the door.

"Fudge! Jordan, I can't meet your parents!" I slid out of the bed and started looking for my clothes.

"Fudge?" he chuckled and stood.

"It's better than what I want to say," I hissed searching around frantically for my clothes. "Where are my damn clothes?"

Relax, Lela," he said, standing up and walking to the door.

"Relax? Seriously, Jordan?"

"What are you freaking out about now?" he asked opening the door, stepping out and stepping back in with my clothes. "Just get dressed and we'll be eating breakfast by the time they get here."

"I have to leave, Jordan!" I hissed pulling the nightshirt off. See, this is why I needed time alone. I was turning into some spastic crazy woman. I was normally calm, cool and collected. This worried, over excitable Lela was not me. I was known for handling things with cool efficiency.

"Uh…why?" Jordan asked sounding choked. I looked up as I pulled on my underwear to see him staring at me. I glanced down at my naked body and back to him.

"Oh, don't look at me like that!" I ordered trying not to be embarrassed. I was in such a panic I had just stripped naked in front of Jordan. I continued putting my clothes on.

"Babe," he said walking over to me and standing in front of me just as I pulled my shirt on. "Calm down. What's wrong?"

"I don't want your parents meeting me with our sex smell all over me, Jordan. It's bad enough everyone else knows."

"Is that what's got you all riled up? I told you last night, I can't smell it anymore since you took the second shower." He placed both hands at my waist and looked down at me. "I'm sure they won't smell it on me either. Now relax."

"I've been in your bed all night, won't they smell that?" I asked and then shook my head incredulously. "I can't believe I'm even having this conversation. Who has a conversation like this?"

"No. They will know we've been around each other a lot. But, your clothes don't smell of me or my bed and it won't be much more than any of the other smells that will accumulate like food smells from the kitchen, animal smells if you pet one of the dogs," he explained patiently. "It's not so highly concentrated since nothing happened between us last night but sleep. Now that they are here however, I think we'd better get in the dining hall and start accumulating some more smells since escape isn't possible for you."

"Great. They're already here?" I whined. I took in a deep breath and let it out slowly. When I spoke again, I at least sounded calmer. "I can't do this, Jordan."

"I can hear a car coming down the drive. If we leave my room now, we can make it to the dining hall before they get in the door," he reassured me.

160

Chapter 23

Turns out, I didn't end up meeting the parents anyway. According to Daisy, Logan had covered for Jordan telling them he was still sleeping after being up for several nights and closing a case early this morning. They had apparently been sequestered in Logan's office catching up on the latest cases as soon as they arrived. After nibbling some fruit and toast, I was ready to go.

Apparently, Logan and Jordan's parents were the founders of Alexander Consulting and Security. Daisy informed me that, although they were basically retired, they stayed on top of the cases and delved in where and when they wanted or were needed.

"Daisy can take me home," I reminded Jordan. "Stay and spend some time with your parents. I can meet them later."

"You'd like that, wouldn't you?" He gave me a narrow – eyed, knowing look.

"I'm not ready for this, Jordan," I whispered to him, a note of pleading in my voice.

"I know," he said against my lips as he bent down to give me a quick kiss. "Will you be ok with Blake? You don't want me to be there when you talk to him?

"No. It would be better if you weren't."

"Daisy do you mind taking Lela home?" He asked, turning to look at Lela who was across the room pretending to be ignoring us.

"Nope. I don't mind at all. Apparently my parents stopped off to see Ethan's folks. So, they won't be home until this evening."

After sending Daisy out to the car ahead of me, Jordan pulled me too him and captured my lips in a toe curling kiss.

"I'll come over tonight," he promised and walked me out to the car.

It was only eleven thirty in the morning and I didn't feel like I'd had enough sleep to deal with Blake. I decided, however, I was in much better shape to deal with Blake than Jordan's parents.

I climbed into the car with Daisy and let out a sigh of relief as we drove away, leaving the ranch behind.

"I know you don't want to talk about it. So, I just want to know is everything ok?" Daisy asked cautiously. "Are you ok?"

"I'm fine. Why does everyone keep asking me that?" It came out grumpier then I'd meant it to.

"A lot has happened in the last twenty – four hours. I just wanted to make sure you are alright," she shrugged. "And, I want you to know you can talk to me if you ever want or need to."

"Thank you." I gave her a grateful smile.

Daisy didn't come in, which was unusual for her. She hadn't said anything else on the ride home either. I suspected she knew I needed some privacy as well as a little me time. She was right. A lot had happened in the last twenty – four hours. I also needed sleep, but that would have to wait until after I talked to Blake. I flinched at the thought. I knew he wouldn't scold or fuss. Nonetheless, for some reason, I feared that I might see disappointment or disapproval in his eyes or words. I wasn't sure if I could take that. I wouldn't dare open my senses. As a matter of fact I made sure they were shut down tight as I opened the front door. At least the bruising around my neck was very faint. The collar on my shirt covered it nicely.

I came in to find Blake making a sandwich in the kitchen. He looked me over thoroughly with an assessing eye.

"Good morning," I said tentatively, feeling awkward and insecure.

"Good morning," he replied. Concern was etched in his face though he was trying his best to hide it. "How are you?"

"I'm fine," I walked over to him and put my arms around him. He immediately wrapped his arms around me and held me close, resting his head on the top of mine.

"Are you sure? Do you want me to make you a sandwich? Are you hungry?"

I smiled against his chest, "No, I'm not hungry. And stop worrying. I really am fine, just extremely tired."

He hesitated but I could tell there was something he wanted to say.

"Will you sit with me for a minute?" he asked, releasing me.

"Of course," I replied feeling lighter now. I didn't need to open my senses to tell he was feeling deep concern for me. That went a long way in making me feel comfortable. We both took a seat at the table.

"You know you can talk to me about anything right?" He was looking into my eyes as if trying to see the answer there.

"I've always known that, Blake," I said sincerely.

"And you know that you don't have to lie to me right?"

"Yes."

"Then why did you lie to me about Jordan? Unless someone else put those hickeys on you?"

"I didn't lie," I said trying not to be mortified. "Everything I told you last night was true. I just left out the part where Jordan gave me the hickeys."

"So you really are helping them with a case?"

"Yes, I am, or was. We closed the case early this morning."

163

"So, I didn't wake up this morning to find you and Jordan gone because I surprised you when I came home early, and you wanted to hide whatever is going on between you two from me?"

"No, Blake." I reached out and touched his hand. "We were able to locate the man and safely rescue him early this morning."

"Oh. Well, that's good news." He sounded somewhat relieved and some of the tension in him seemed to ease. "You know this is your home right?"

"Yes. I know that," I answered quizzically as his tone became serious and his gaze searching again.

"As much as I hate the idea of you with Jordan, or any man for that matter, I'm trying really hard to be realistic. I want you to be happy here. And, I don't want you to think that you have to sneak around trying to hide your relationships from me like some teenager. This is your home and you should feel comfortable here. Though, I don't want to wake up each day I'm here to find Jordan here."

"You won't. And, I'm not hiding anything from you. It's just all so new between Jordan and me. I honestly don't know where we stand."

"What do you mean, you don't know where you stand?" he asked sounding a bit incredulous and big brotherly. "Obviously close enough to leave hickey's on you. Please don't tell me this is some casual thing you guys have going on."

"Your inner big brother is showing," I teased. "No, it's not some casual thing. It's just new. And, I'm not totally sure how I feel about it all yet."

"How does Jordan feel?"

"He's very sure about how he feels and what he wants. I just wasn't looking to get involved with anyone, yet here I am," I shrugged and

164

looked away. Blake didn't say anything and when I swung my gaze back to him he was watching me speculatively. When he finally spoke his voice was almost a whisper and held a note of something I couldn't identify.

"Give him a chance, Lela."

"I – I am," I confided in surprise.

"If he happens to be here when I come home sometimes or wake up in the morning, I'll just try not to be creeped out," he grimaced. He'd obviously had a hard time saying the words. I appreciated him all the more for saying them.

"It would be just as weird for me. Trust me that's something you won't have to worry about," I muttered, flushing to my toes.

"Jordan seems like a good guy from the little I've seen of him. The whole family seems really wonderful," he added with a lot less difficulty.

"They are wonderful people," I agreed.

He nodded. "Ok. Well just know, I am always here for you."

"I know you are," I smiled, then leaned over to give him a hug and kiss on the cheek.

Chapter 24

Daisy was back at two -thirty in the afternoon under the pretense that she was filling me in on the meeting with Logan. Logan had already called saying he figured I was too tired to sit in on the meeting but assured me that Mr. Beck and his family were reunited last night within two hours of his rescue. He told me he would fill me in on the meeting when he saw me next if I wanted him to or if Jordan, Ethan or Daisy hadn't already done it. Daisy took it upon herself to take on the task. She told me that Mr. Beck was safely at home, which I already knew from Logan. The authorities had swooped in and taken over the property where Mr. Beck had been held. Of course any drainers scattered like roaches. They could not be discovered by the regular authorities. It was in their best interest to guard their secret so that was always the first priority. And now Alexander Consulting had a lot more information on this organization. They hadn't been able to get Kevin's superior, but they put his organization in a tailspin. Kevin was most likely a definite target. He knew too much, and they had to suspect that he had something to do with the success of this mission. So his security had been stepped up. The idea of Kevin becoming an asset was somewhat disconcerting, however, I couldn't deny that he could be with his vast experience with his drainer crime organization. He could really help out in bringing them down if he could be flipped.

Daisy had decided to hang out for a while, but I was too exhausted to be of much company. I did notice, however, that she didn't have any problem at all keeping Blake company. Over the last few weeks since I'd met Daisy, I noticed that there seemed to be some sort of attraction going on between Blake and Daisy. Blake had only been home for a couple of weekends. Daisy was around a lot anyway, however, she was always around whenever Blake was home. I couldn't help noticing though that she tended to stay late if she went home at all when Blake was around. And today while I napped, they'd left me sleeping and went swimming in the pool together. Their laughter and splashing filtered in the window as I dozed. I wasn't sure how I felt about the possibility of Blake and Daisy hooking up, but decided I had enough to think about with Jordan. I couldn't worry too much over Daisy and Blake.

Surprisingly, Daisy didn't stay that night. She said her parents would also be home that evening and she wanted to spend time with them. She promised to come back tomorrow though. I let John know I wouldn't be in the office on Monday. I had full intentions on sleeping in and having a three day weekend to rest up from the past week. I went to bed early, leaving Blake to watch television by himself.

Sometime in the night, I woke to find Jordan watching me. He was lying beside me on his side, facing me and propped on his elbow.

"What are you doing here?" I asked sleepily, frowning.

"Watching you sleep," he smiled back.

"Didn't I already tell you that was creepy," I mumbled, closing my eyes again.

"Yes," he chuckled. "You did."

Then I felt his lips touch mine. The kisses started out soft and sweet. I reached up, threading my fingers in his hair and he deepened the kiss. I could feel desire rising as he slowly consumed my mouth and his hands began to wonder my body. The thought of Blake in the next room had me putting on the breaks.

"Jordan, we can't do this," I mumbled against his lips, breaking the kiss.

"If you could be quiet we could," he spoke into my neck as he trailed kisses there. "You're so loud though, I'm surprised your neighbors don't hear you."

"I am not loud!" I tried to hiss, but it came out kind of breathy and choked as he was driving me crazy nibbling on my neck.

"Ok. I was just kidding about the neighbors." He looked up grinning at me. "But, honestly, you are rather loud once I get you going. You give off these sexy moans and –"

"Jordan." I cut him off and put a hand over his lips. He reached up and took my hand away from his mouth and held it. He gazed down at me and for a moment neither of us spoke.

167

"Can I sleep with you tonight," he asked breaking the intimate silence between us. "Just sleep. I promise. I meant it when I said we're going to take it slow."

"Blake doesn't want to see you in the mornings when he wakes up here," I whispered.

"I don't blame him. I don't want to wake up and see him, either," he frowned. "I don't want him looking at me sideways wondering what I've been doing all night with his little sister. Don't worry. He'll never know I'm here. Just like he didn't when we were protecting you."

I gave in reluctantly. I loved the feel of Jordan sleeping next to me and that made me nervous.

"Fine. As long as this isn't an every night thing."

"Whenever you don't want me to stay, I won't stay," he promised. He bent down to give me another sweet kiss then rolled to his side and pulled me to him. "Now go back to sleep."

"Jordan, about your parents," I began.

"I told you we can take it slow. That includes my parents," he assured me. "You don't have to meet them until you're ready. They'll be gone soon anyway."

"You're ok with me not meeting them now?"

"I'm perfectly fine with it. Now go to sleep, Lela, and stop thinking and worrying," he murmured into my hair.

"I don't want you to think I don't want to meet them ever. I just don't want to meet them now," I explained, wanting to make sure he wasn't offended.

"Lela?"

"Yes?"

"Either shut up and go to sleep or I'm going to think you'd rather stay awake. I can think of much more pleasurable things to do than talk if you want to stay awake."

"Fine!"

And with that, I closed my eyes and drifted off to sleep in the comfort and warmth of Jordan's arms.

The following is an excerpt from <u>Deep in the Night</u>, book 3 of the Alexander Ranch series available now

Deep in the Night

An Alexander Ranch Matter # 3

By Marla Josephs

Cover photo by Beverly Fields and Amado Temporal

© **Tempfield Press and Beverly Fields 2014**

To my husband, my partner in all things. Thanks for everything. You are the best. And to my children, you are my inspiration.

Prologue

"Come here, doggy."

The dog came warily closer to the hand holding out a piece of bread.

"That's it. Come on," the soothing voice crooned.

Finally deciding that everything was safe, the dog gave into his desire for the bread and gradually took it from the outstretched hand. After gulping that piece down in one bite, the dog was handed another and another. When all the bread was gone, the dog lay down and allowed the stranger to pet his head. He soon grew sleepy and fell into a deep, soothing sleep. The next morning when the dog's owner called to him, he did not respond.

"Bear! Bear!" the boy called out over and over again. But, Bear did not come. When the boy finally walked around to the side of the house where the dog run was, he saw the dog lying on the ground sleeping. That was odd, thought the boy. Bear wasn't usually asleep at this time. And, even if he was, he would have awakened at hearing his name. The boy sank down next to the dog and pet him gently along his back. Then he stiffened. Something was very wrong. Bear's body felt deathly still.

"Bear?" the boy said placing his hand on the animal's side and then quickly drawing it away. He stood up so abruptly he stumbled backward.

"Mom! M-o-o-o-m! Something's wrong with Bear!" he yelled as he ran towards the house. Bear lay still, never to move again.

Chapter 1

Why is it that the first days back from a vacation are always the busiest? Yet, they are probably the days you are least mentally prepared for work? I was now sitting in my office after a long day reminiscing about the relaxing vacation I'd just had. Prior to said vacation, I'd had a long, back and forth debate with myself about where to go on vacation. In the end, my brother Blake and I had agreed to an all-inclusive, eight day vacation in Puerta Vallarta, Mexico. Blake had originally left the decision to me. However, he'd had to step in when I couldn't seem to make up my mind. We ended up agreeing that we wanted something like a staycation...just not at home.

Though Puerta Vallarta had a lot to do, we'd been there several times before. Hanging out at the pool, relaxing, eating, and snoozing in the Mexican shade sounded just fine for now. If we had gone somewhere else, we wouldn't have been able to force ourselves to relax. Blake, however, was tired of travelling and didn't want to spend his vacation going on excursion after excursion each day. He travelled constantly for work, and I simply worked all the time. We needed a restful vacation.

So, we had a nice, relaxing vacation with only a few excursions. Blake parasailed one afternoon from the beach in front of our resort while I videotaped. Our busiest day was the second day we were there. We decided to do two excursions on the same day. We swam with the dolphins by day and enjoyed a rousing pirate dinner cruise on the Marigalante by night. Swimming with the dolphins was always so much fun. It just wouldn't have been complete without that and the Marigalante.

The Marigalante is an exact replica of Columbus' Santa Maria. Besides the beautiful views of Puerto Vallarta and Banderas Bay from the ship, the crew put on a heck of a pirate show. The entertainment included one of the performers diving off the ship into the water in the dark of night and a fireworks show. The food wasn't too shabby either. Actually, it was downright delicious. No matter how many times we visited Puerta Vallarta, we never missed these two excursions. They were a must do.

The only other excursion we had was a trip to do some shopping. For Blake and I, that was probably the most subdued vacation we'd ever been on. And now, I was back at work wishing that I'd booked it for a little longer and taken just a few more days off. Perhaps I was becoming less of a workaholic.

Being on vacation had been a heck of a lot better than trying to figure out what was going on with our client's animals. Several of our clients had brought their dogs to us close to death, or dead, with no obvious cause of death. None of them had survived. We probably wouldn't have thought much of it if only one or two clients had come in. But, apparently these mysterious deaths had started while I was on vacation. In the last nine days, five cases had found their way to our veterinary clinic.

After being investigated by our vet staff, poisoning was ruled out via blood tests. Each owner had been question regarding the food they fed their pets. Each dog was fed a different brand of food according to the owners, which ruled out a food born outbreak from a specific manufacturer. Currently we were stumped. Now, we were contemplating having the bodies sent out for necropsy or sending out tissue samples to determine some other toxicological reason. For now, we were advising our pet owners to keep a close eye on their pets and keep their animals with them at all times. Realizing I was now frowning at my latest thoughts about our suspicious pet deaths, I moved to shut my computer down just as my phone rang. It was Jordan.

Jordan was my...boyfriend? We hadn't exactly defined our relationship. After a rocky beginning that included me getting shot, him saving me, some hot steamy kisses mixed with a lot of reluctance on my part, we finally settled on dating.

"Hey," I said smiling in anticipation of his voice. I hadn't heard that voice in almost two weeks while I was on vacation. I'd missed it.

"I missed you," he said in his low, rich tone. That tone that never failed to cause the flutters in my stomach.

"I missed you too," I said impishly. I knew what was coming next, and I was trying to hide my laughter in anticipation.

"Are you sure, Lela?" he asked, his voice taking on a tone that was a cross between disgruntled and sarcastic. "You didn't call me when you got in last night like I asked you to."

"It was late, Jordan," I said trying to reason with him. I really had missed Jordan. But, I'd been exhausted when Blake and I had returned late. And, if I had called Jordan to let him know I was home, he'd have shown up on my doorstep, or more accurately, in my bed. I was half surprised I hadn't found him there this morning.

"I told you I didn't care what time you got in. I would have still come over," he explained earnestly.

"I know, Jordan," I groaned. "That's what I was afraid of."

"See, I knew you didn't miss me," he feigned a pout.

"I did. I told you so this morning when I texted you that I was on my way to work," I chided. "I was really tired. We got in really late. If you had come over, I wouldn't have gotten enough sleep to get to work this morning."

"You're always tired," he commented grumpily. "You need some Geritol or something."

"Oh…, wow. Thanks!" I shot back sardonically. "I'm so sorry I don't have super human energy and strength like you. How dare I need eight hours of sleep regularly."

"Seriously, Lela. You sleep more than the average person," he went on, warming to his topic.

"Uh, Jordan?"

"Hm?" came his smug voice.

"I'm thinking maybe you don't get to come over tonight either," I said sweetly.

"Ok, ok. I'm just messing with you," he said easily. "Are you headed home now?"

"I just shut my computer down."

"I'll meet you there."

Blake wasn't home when I arrived, but Jordan was sitting in the driveway in his Aston Martin when I pulled in. I'd barely turned the engine off before he was there opening my door with a big grin on his face. The moment I was out of the car he pulled me into his arms for an urgent kiss. As usual, that was all it took for me to melt into him.

"We are going to dinner," he announced in a voice that brooked no argument when he finally released my mouth. "Do you need to change clothes or anything?"

I didn't. I was the Facilities Director for Hanley's Pet Care Services. Although I was a registered vet tech, I almost never worked in that capacity. My job was to make all of the various departments run smoothly at our facilities. We had pet grooming, training, boarding and veterinary care services. I made it all work seamlessly for the needs of our clients. Since I'd been buried by all of the paperwork that went along with my job today, I hadn't had a moment to even visit the actual facilities where animal interaction took place. Being animal hair and germ free, there was no need for me to change.

"Actually, I'm starving. And, no. I don't need to change clothes. I'll just text Blake on the way and let him know I've gone out to dinner with you."

I hit the button on the key fob to lock my car and climbed into the passenger side of his car where Jordan was holding the door for me.

"The Aston Martin tonight?" I asked with a raised brow when he climbed in beside me on the driver's side.

"You are mine tonight," he stated and then frowned. "Well, at least you are for a little while. I know you won't come back to the ranch with me, and I know you won't be totally mine tonight at your house with Blake there. So, I figured I'd take you to dinner to get you to myself for a few hours."

"Sounds good," I laughed. "Just remember it's a work night."

"Don't worry. I'll have you home in time to get your beauty rest," he teased.

Jordan pulled up in front of our favorite Italian restaurant right on the water. My stomach grumbled loudly and my mouth began to water.

"Il Pescatore?" I asked excitedly.

"I knew you'd like this," Jordan said smugly.

"Heck yea!" I exclaimed enthusiastically. "You have to make sure I save room for the tiramisu."

"If you don't, we can always take it to go," he shrugged with a knowing grin.

My hunger pangs became more insistent once we entered the restaurant and all of the wonderful smells teased my nose.

175

"So, how was your first day back?" Jordan asked once we were seated.

"Busy!" I declared. "And, I was *so* not into it today. Though, I had no choice but to make myself dive in head first. There's so much to do. And, we've got a problem that we can't seem to figure out."

"What kind of problem?" Jordan murmured looking over the menu.

"Apparently, while I was gone, several clients brought their dogs in wondering why their previously healthy dogs seemed to just drop dead. Looking over their records, all of them came in for their regular checkups and were in great shape. None of the prior exams indicated these dogs were anything but healthy."

"What do you mean, just dropped dead?" Jordan asked looking up from his menu.

"I mean, they just dropped dead," I exclaimed definitively. "Each of the owners just found their dog dead, or close to it, in the morning. No wounds, evidence of a fight, or injury. If it had been one or two then we'd have assumed it was a coincidence."

"How many have there been?" Jordan was now looking very interested.

"Apparently, there have been five in the last nine days. And, one more came in today. It's crazy. We were starting to suspect that someone might be poisoning them. John approved the vets doing blood work to test for poison while I was gone. The results came back today and there is no sign of poisoning. We just can't figure it out. We are thinking of sending them out for some necropsies, or at least checking the tissues for other toxicology or organ failure."

Jordan was looking thoughtful. Before I could question him, however, our waitress came to take our orders. I ordered a much needed glass of wine along with a seafood ravioli entre. Jordan ordered a combination platter that he would undoubtedly eat every bite of and still have room for dessert.

"So, there haven't been any clear signs of cause of death? No evidence of any type of fight or struggle?" Jordan asked, repeating my words once the waitress walked away to put our orders in.

"No. Nothing. According to each of the owners, the dogs seemed to just be sleeping peacefully."

"Do you think Grace could take a look at the corpses?" Jordan was frowning now. His question had me almost choking on my water. "Grace? Why?"

"I don't know," he said pensively. "We've caught a case that we are finding rather strange as well. They don't seem to be related, yet I feel like we should check it out."

"What kind of case?"

"We've had two men drained very violently in the last week and a half. And, while this isn't necessarily an unusual occurrence, they were both found dead in their cars not very far away from each other. We don't know where they were drained, but they don't have anything in common. And, they didn't live anywhere near each other, or where they were dumped. Normally a drainer would not bother to drive their victims anywhere after killing them. At most, they would make only minimal effort to hide the body."

"So, you think my dead dogs might have something to do with your dead men?" I asked skeptically.

"No, not necessarily. However, it sounds like your dogs may have been drained. So, we should probably not overlook these strange deaths. It's still an unusual death for a drained dog. Most drainers who kill animals don't care if they brutally drain them. They usually wouldn't do it close enough to their homes to leave the bodies where the owners could find them. Like you said, maybe if it were one here and there it wouldn't be cause for suspicion. But, five dogs killed the same way in a matter of days is a pattern."

Our waitress brought our food then, cutting off our conversation.

"Enough shop talk," Jordan said once our waitress walked away. "Tell me all about Mexico and how you were too busy to even miss me."

"I wasn't too busy to miss you," I laughed. "Actually, I missed you very much."

"Sure," Jordan grumbled pretending disbelief. "Just tell me about all the fun you had."

Look for <u>Deep in the Night</u> and other books by Marla Josephs at Amazon, Barnes and Noble, and Ibooks.

Check out more titles by Marla Josephs at:

www.marlajosephs.com

www.ingramcontent.com/pod-product-compliance
Lightning Source LLC
Chambersburg PA
CBHW060423130626
46555CB00005B/2192